# The Canyon Ascent

A Torlan Tarsen Adventure

# The Canyon Ascent

Russell V McFall

*Ordained Path Books*

This is a work of fiction. Names, characters, places, and incidents are the product of the author's imagination or are used fictitiously. Any resemblance to actual persons, living or dead, events, or locales is entirely coincidental.

Published by **Ordained Path Books**
For permissions or inquiries, contact:
**ordainedpathbooks@gmail.com**

Cover illustration and interior artwork generated by AI under direction of the author.

**First Edition**

**ISBN (Paperback): 978-1-972724-10-1**
**ISBN (Hardcover): 978-1-972724-12-5**

Printed in the United States of America.

Version 1.01 -- April 2026

## Dedication

*For those who trust the path set before them,*
*even when it disappears into the unknown—*
*may you find strength for each step*
*and peace in the One who guides the way.*

# Contents

Dedication ....................vii
Chapter 1 - The Final Site ....................1
Chapter 2 - Through Motion ....................14
Chapter 3 - Return to Meridian....................21
Chapter 4 - In Transit ....................29
Chapter 5 - The Incident ....................38
Chapter 6 - First Minutes ....................47
Chapter 7 – Triage....................55
Chapter 8 - Securing the Site ....................64
Chapter 9 - First Night....................72
Chapter 10 - Morning Assessment....................81
Chapter 11 - First Signal ....................89
Chapter 12 - Signal Failure ....................96
Chapter 13 - Fredrick's Passing ....................104
Chapter 14 - The Argument ....................112
Chapter 15 - The Night Pressure ....................119
Chapter 16 - Morning Evidence ....................128
Chapter 17 - Route Scouting ....................135
Chapter 18 - First Movement....................143
Chapter 19 - The Carry....................151
Chapter 20 - The Narrow Pass ....................159
Chapter 21 - Forced Pause ....................167
Chapter 22 - Ledge Camp....................174
Chapter 23 - Final Push ....................181
Chapter 24 - The Plateau ....................189
Chapter 25 - Establishing the Plateau ....................196
Chapter 26 - Signal Refinement ....................202
Chapter 27 - Plateau Pressure ....................208
Chapter 28 - The Search Tightens ....................214
Chapter 29 - The Waiting Line ....................219
Chapter 30 - The Extraction Begins....................225
Chapter 31 - The Ride Back ....................231
Chapter 32 - Arrival....................236
Chapter 33 – Recovery....................241

Chapter 34 - The Report ....................................................................247
Epilogue - After the Climb....................................................................253
Author's Note ....................................................................259
A Torlan Tarsen Adventure ....................................................................261
Appendix — Canyon Incident Summary ....................................................................262
About the Author....................................................................265
Also by Russell McFall ....................................................................266

## Chapter 1 - The Final Site

The shuttle came in low over the broken ridges of Virella, its shadow slipping across stone and scrub in a long dark shape that bent and stretched over the uneven ground below. Beyond the forward glass, the land opened in layers of muted color—gray-brown rock, dark mineral shelves, sparse bands of hardy vegetation clinging where the soil was thick enough to hold, and farther off, the pale blue haze that always seemed to hang over the distant valleys of this world.

Alex Hale sat forward in her seat, one hand resting lightly against the edge of the console as she studied the settlement ahead. "That has to be it," she said.

William Arden glanced up from the tablet in his lap. He had already finished reading the latest equipment report several minutes earlier, but he had kept it open, going back over the numbers in silence while the shuttle descended. That was his way. He rarely rushed to speak. He preferred to let information settle into place first, to see what held together and what did not.

Below them, the final communications site on their route came into view.

It was smaller than Outpost Meridian, smaller than any of the six settlements they had visited in the past two weeks, and it looked as if it had been built more from necessity than ambition. A cluster of low utility buildings sat against the base of a long rise of dark stone. A landing pad had been cut into the flatter ground nearby, though "cut" was perhaps too generous a word. It looked more as though someone had found the least broken stretch of rock and declared it good enough. To one side stood the communications mast they had come to repair—tall, narrow, and slightly angled against the wind, with three relay dishes mounted at different heights and a secondary lattice running down one side like a crude attempt to solve a problem after the fact.

Fredrick Mercer leaned toward the front glass from the seat across the aisle and gave a tired little breath that was almost a laugh. "That," he said, "is the one I was hoping you'd tell me we could skip."

Alex smiled faintly. "Too late for that now."

Fredrick settled back with a hand pressed against his knee. He was in his early sixties, broad-shouldered once but softened a little by years behind consoles and workstations instead of out in the field. There was still something solid about him, though. He had the look of a man who had spent most of his life being dependable and had been leaned on so often that he no longer knew how not to be. William had seen that quality in him from the beginning. Fredrick knew the colony's communications systems as well as anyone on Virella. He knew the hardware, the procedures, the maintenance cycles, the best placements, the worst weather seasons, the signal relay schedules, and all the tricks that should have worked.

The trouble was, on Virella, they often didn't.

The pilot banked slightly and brought the shuttle into alignment with the landing pad. A crosswind tapped at the hull, then steadied. Below, several figures were already gathering near the edge of the pad, their faces turned upward. Some stood with arms folded, others with hands on hips, and more than one carried the look William had seen before at the other sites: not hope exactly, but a careful kind of guarded interest. Too many people had already come promising solutions.

The shuttle settled with a low hiss of displaced dust and a soft jolt through the deck.

Fredrick unclipped his harness and muttered, "Well. Let's go disappoint or impress them."

Alex gave him a look. "You're very encouraging."

"I'm realistic," Fredrick said.

William rose, tucked the tablet under his arm, and reached automatically for the equipment case stowed beside his seat. Alex was already ahead of him, lifting the heavier field kit and slinging its strap over one shoulder with practiced ease.

"I've got that," William said.

"I know," she replied, without looking at him. "I also know it's mine."

There was no challenge in her voice. There rarely was. She simply stated things as they were and kept moving. William followed her toward the hatch, and Fredrick, seeing the exchange, shook his head in mild amusement.

"You know," Fredrick said quietly as they waited for the hatch to cycle open, "most assistants don't answer a man like that."

Alex looked back over one shoulder. "Good thing I'm not most assistants."

Fredrick smiled. William said nothing, but there was the faintest shift at the corner of his mouth.

The hatch lowered, and dry wind swept into the shuttle carrying the mineral scent of hot stone and machine dust. Outside, the waiting group stepped forward. There were seven of them: site operators, technicians, and one woman whose expression said she had already decided not to trust the visit until proven necessary. William approved of that. Skepticism wasted less time than false optimism.

Fredrick was first down the ramp. He always seemed to know how to bridge the space between technical problem and human concern, not by talking too much, but by putting people at ease before the real work began.

"Morning," he called as he stepped onto the pad. "I know, I know. You were all hoping I'd come back with a miracle."

A narrow-faced man in a dust-marked utility jacket answered him. "At this point we'd settle for stable transmission after dusk."

Fredrick nodded once. "Then perhaps we can improve your standards later. For now, let's start there." He turned slightly and motioned toward William. "This is William Arden."

A few faces changed at the name. William noticed it immediately. One or two had heard it before. That had happened more often as the trip continued. The first settlements had met him with polite reserve. The later ones had been waiting. Word moved even when the network did not.

Fredrick continued. "And this is Alex Hale. If you're wise, you'll assume she already knows what you were about to say before you say it."

That brought a few guarded smiles.

The woman with the skeptical expression stepped forward first. "Dena Corlin," she said. "Site supervisor."

William inclined his head. "Good to meet you."

She glanced from him to the equipment cases and then to Fredrick. "We've had two different teams here in the last four months. One from Meridian. One contracted out from Lethen Ridge. They both said the same thing: the mast was structurally sound, the dishes were aligned, and the local amplifiers were within tolerance.

Then they adjusted everything twice and left, and the signal was still dropping every time the weather shifted or the evening fog settled in."

"They weren't wrong," William said.

That seemed to catch her slightly off guard. "Excuse me?"

"They weren't wrong," he repeated. "The mast probably is structurally sound. The dishes are likely aligned. The amplifiers probably are within tolerance. That doesn't mean the system is properly tuned to this site."

Dena studied him for a second longer, then folded her arms. "You're saying the equipment isn't broken."

"I'm saying that if you keep trying to solve this as a hardware failure, you'll keep getting temporary improvements and permanent disappointment."

Fredrick made a quiet sound in the back of his throat, something halfway between satisfaction and relief. He had heard William say the same thing in different forms at nearly every site on the planet.

Alex had already set the field kit down on a flat section of pad and was opening the latches. "Do you have your site logs for the last ten days?" she asked.

Dena looked at her. "Yes."

"Signal strength by hour?"

"Yes."

"Ground conductivity tests?"

A pause. "Some."

Alex nodded as if that answer had been expected. "We'll start with what you have."

There was something about the way she said it that removed unnecessary friction from the moment. She did not sound demanding. She sounded prepared. William had seen people underestimate her only once, maybe twice. They did not usually make that mistake again.

Within minutes they were inside the main communications building.

The room was functional and spare, like most structures on Virella. The walls were reinforced composite over local stone. The consoles were arranged in a narrow arc facing a series of screens that displayed relay status, atmospheric data, power balance, and signal fluctuation graphs. On the far wall hung a topographic map of the surrounding region, marked with hand-added notations where the official grid had proved too optimistic to be useful.

William paused just inside the doorway and let his eyes move over the whole room.

That, more than anything else, was often the beginning of his work.

He did not head immediately for the central console. He did not ask the nearest technician to summarize the problem in a rush of defensive detail. He looked. He listened. He watched the signal graph tremble slightly even now, in broad daylight, when the system should have been at its best. He noted the relay timing, the delay between the primary tower and the secondary repeater, the atmospheric density readings, the small adjustments someone had made by hand to compensate for a recurring drift. He glanced once at the wall map and saw the ridgeline to the west, the shallow basin south of the settlement, and the narrow low region where cooler air likely collected in the evenings.

Then he walked to the main station.

"Show me your drop pattern after local sunset," he said.

One of the younger technicians pulled up the record. It was almost exactly what William expected to see: signal decay that was too regular to be random, too site-specific to be systemwide, and too sensitive to terrain and moisture conditions to be solved by standard amplification alone.

Fredrick moved beside him. "This is where the others kept trying to compensate," he said, pointing to the graph. "They boosted output here and here, adjusted the handoff delay there, ran shielding modifications, even replaced the phase stabilizer."

"And it helped for a few hours," William said.

Fredrick looked at him. "Yes."

Alex was at the secondary console now, sorting local reports into a cleaner sequence and discarding two pages of unnecessary explanatory notes that someone had attached to the maintenance file. "Ground conductivity readings are inconsistent," she said. "Not wildly. Just enough."

William turned his attention to the mast diagram. "Not inconsistent," he said after a moment. "Contextual."

The younger technician frowned. "I'm not sure what that means."

William stepped back from the console and looked toward the window that faced the tower itself. "It means your system isn't malfunctioning in isolation. It's responding to the site. The terrain below this ridge is holding density longer in the evening than your current relay shift accounts for. The atmospheric scatter isn't arriving from one direction. It's rising and pooling from below. Your relay handoff is timed for open-air dissipation, but this site doesn't dissipate the way the system assumes it does."

The room went quiet.

Fredrick did not smile this time. He only lowered his gaze once, as if some part of him was still adjusting to the fact that the problem really had not been beyond understanding after all—only beyond the framework they had been using to interpret it.

Dena Corlin stepped closer. "Can you fix it?"

William looked at the mast again. "Yes."

It was not said with pride. It was said the way a carpenter might say a beam needed to be cut shorter.

Alex closed one file and opened another. "Then we should start with the lower grounding lattice and the timing offset," she said. "If the evening density builds upward from the basin, the system needs to anticipate that shift instead of reacting to it."

William glanced at her. "Yes."

Dena noticed the exchange and seemed, for the first time, to understand the shape of the partnership standing in front of her.

For the next two hours the building became a place of purposeful motion.

William went up the mast himself for the first adjustment, which drew the expected reaction from the settlement crew. He could have asked one of the local technicians to do it. He simply did not see the point. It was faster to confirm the dish angle and grounding structure firsthand than to explain every detail up and down the line. He moved with calm efficiency, clipped in where required, carrying a toolkit that seemed smaller than it should have been in his large hands. Wind pressed against his jacket as he reached the upper relay bracket and paused there, looking out over the settlement and the stone country beyond.

Virella stretched outward in long broken lines, beautiful in a hard, restrained way. From above, he could see the basin that had likely contributed to the problem, the slow contour of the ridges, and the way the land dipped just enough to trap cool air when evening came. The answer had always been there. The planet was not hiding it. People had simply been trying to force the site to behave like somewhere else.

Below him, Alex coordinated from the ground with crisp, efficient clarity. "Two degrees left," she called. "Hold. Now lower the secondary phase delay by point-three."

William made the adjustment. "Done."

Fredrick stood near the outer relay console, watching the stabilization numbers settle. He had seen enough now to stop being surprised each time William recognized the deeper pattern behind a problem, but the admiration had not lessened. If anything, it had deepened. There was relief in it too. On this world, where distances were great and small failures multiplied into larger ones, relief mattered.

The final correction was not dramatic. It rarely was.

William came down from the mast, crossed directly to the secondary console, and adjusted the relay anticipation window by a narrow margin that seemed too small to matter until the signal graph on the center screen flattened into a steadier line than anyone in the room had seen in months.

No one spoke for three full seconds.

Then one of the younger operators said quietly, "That's not averaging."

"No," Alex said, studying the return. "It isn't."

Dena stepped to the transmission panel. "Meridian relay check," she said into the mic, voice controlled but slightly tighter than before. "Final site requesting live confirmation. Meridian relay check."

The room listened.

For half a second there was only static.

Then a voice came back, clean enough to make two people in the room actually straighten where they stood.

"Meridian receiving clearly. Repeat, receiving clearly. Signal strength stable. What changed out there?"

Dena looked at William, then at Fredrick, then gave a short disbelieving laugh that carried more exhaustion than amusement. "Apparently," she said into the mic, "we finally stopped fighting the planet long enough to listen to it."

Fredrick let out a breath and rubbed one hand over his face. "I may borrow that line."

"You may not," Dena said, still looking at the console.

Alex was already noting final settings and local training points. "We'll want your evening test repeated at three intervals," she said. "Don't assume midday stability means the shift is complete. The pattern should hold after dusk now, but you need to verify it."

Dena turned to her. "You've done this before."

Alex gave the smallest hint of a smile. "Several times this week."

That loosened the room further. A tension nobody had wanted to acknowledge began to drain away. One technician leaned back against the console and shook his head. Another gave Fredrick a look that was half accusation and half gratitude for not giving up when the earlier teams had failed.

William gathered the diagnostic slate and looked once more at the live graph. It held steady.

He did not feel triumph. He never quite did in moments like this. Satisfaction, perhaps. More often something quieter than that. A sense that the world had made sense again, at least in one place, and that this was how it should be.

Fredrick came to stand beside him. "I asked for you because I thought you might see what the rest of us weren't seeing," he said softly.

William kept his eyes on the graph. "You saw enough to know the problem had been framed wrong."

Fredrick gave a short shrug. "That and a great deal of frustration."

"That still counts."

Fredrick looked at him, and his expression warmed. "You know, you make it very hard for a man to be properly dramatic."

"That has been mentioned before," William said.

Alex closed the final log file and sealed the equipment case. "We can leave as soon as they finish the next two checks."

Dena overheard that. "You're not staying through evening?"

William turned toward her. "The system should hold. If it doesn't, Fredrick has the adjustment sequence, and Alex's notes are more organized than mine."

"That's not difficult," Alex said.

Fredrick gave a quiet chuckle. "True enough."

But Dena was still studying William. "You trust your work that much?"

William glanced toward the window, where the mast stood against the pale Virellan sky. "I trust that this site is now working with its environment instead of against it."

Dena considered that, then nodded once. "Fair enough."

Outside, the wind had eased. The hard light of afternoon lay across the settlement in long, flat planes, and the ridges beyond looked softer from this angle, though William knew better than to trust distance to make anything on Virella truly gentle.

They remained for another hour, walking the local crew through the adjusted settings, explaining not just what had changed but why. That mattered to William. Fixing a problem once was useful. Leaving people able to understand it afterward was better.

Alex handled much of the practical training. By now she could move through the revised system almost as naturally as William could, and in some ways more clearly, because she translated without losing precision. Fredrick noticed that too. More than once that afternoon he stepped back and simply watched her work.

At one point, while the others were occupied at the primary console, he came to stand near William at the open doorway.

"She's good," he said quietly.

William looked across the room toward Alex. "Yes."

Fredrick folded his arms loosely. "Better than good."

William said nothing.

Fredrick glanced sideways at him. "You know, most men with your reputation would have come alone, solved the problem, and left everyone else behind trying to catch up."

"She didn't need to catch up."

"No," Fredrick said. "She didn't."

There was no teasing in his voice. Only approval.

By the time the final verification came through from Meridian, the settlement's mood had shifted completely. The skepticism was gone. Relief had taken its place, not loud or celebratory, but deep enough to be felt in the way people stood, the way shoulders settled, the way voices lowered back to ordinary levels after weeks of irritation and repeated failure.

Fredrick accepted their thanks with the modest discomfort of a man who did not feel he deserved most of it.

William accepted it even more quietly.

Alex accepted it, then redirected half of it toward the local operators who would now be maintaining the system themselves.

It was nearly evening when they walked back toward the shuttle.

The light had changed. On Virella, evening did not arrive in warmth. It arrived in a slow cooling that seemed to draw itself upward from the low ground, touching the base of the ridges first and then creeping out over the open stretches. William noticed a faint gathering haze in the basin to the south and paused for one moment to watch it.

Fredrick saw him looking. "You're doing it again."

William turned slightly. "Doing what?"

"Thinking past the problem we just solved."

Alex adjusted the field kit on her shoulder. "He does that a lot."

Fredrick smiled. "Yes. I've noticed."

William gave the basin one final look, then followed them up the ramp.

Behind them, the mast stood straight against the evening sky, sending clean signal out across the harsh and difficult world of Virella.

For the first time in a long while, this site was connected.

And for the first time that day, with the work finished and the return journey finally in front of them, the three of them allowed themselves the smallest measure of quiet.

Tomorrow, they would head back toward Outpost Meridian.

The job was done.

At least, that was how it seemed.

## Chapter 2 - Through Motion

The shuttle lifted from the final site just as the last of the evening haze began to gather along the low ground.

From above, the change was easier to see.

What had looked like nothing from the surface—just a soft dimming of distance—revealed itself as a slow, deliberate layering of air. The basin to the south filled first, pale and indistinct, and then the thin edge of it crept outward, touching the base of the ridges and lingering there as though the land itself were holding it in place.

Alex watched it through the side glass as the shuttle climbed. "It starts earlier here," she said.

William followed her gaze. "Yes."

Fredrick leaned slightly forward from his seat. "You noticed that on the logs too?"

William nodded. "The drop pattern begins before the readings show it. The environment shifts first. The system reacts second."

Fredrick let out a quiet breath. "We kept treating it like the system was failing on its own."

"You were responding to what you could measure," William said. "The problem was in what you weren't measuring."

Fredrick sat back again, one hand resting loosely on his knee. "That's a difficult thing to admit after thirty years working communications."

Alex glanced at him. "It's also why you knew to call him."

Fredrick gave her a brief look, then nodded once. "Fair enough."

The shuttle leveled out as it gained altitude, the ground below resolving into broader patterns. The settlement they had just left became a small cluster against the rock, the mast now only a thin line, and beyond it the land stretched in long, uneven layers. From this height, the network of settlements made more sense. Each one had been placed with intention—near resources, along manageable terrain, within range of relay lines that should have worked cleanly across open air.

Should have.

Alex shifted in her seat and pulled up the route map on her console. The twelve settlements of the Meridian network appeared as a scattered pattern across the region, connected by faint lines that represented communication paths rather than physical roads. Some of those lines had been steady when they arrived on Virella. Others had flickered in and out of reliability. A few had failed entirely depending on time of day, atmospheric conditions, or terrain.

Now, most of them were stable.

"Eight sites," Alex said, tapping lightly at the display. "We've adjusted eight. The rest were already functioning within acceptable range."

Fredrick nodded. "The central ring around Outpost Meridian held up well enough. It was the outer settlements that gave us trouble."

William looked at the map. "Elevation variance is higher on the outer ring."

"Yes," Fredrick said. "We knew that."

William's eyes moved from one site to another. "But you treated each site independently."

Fredrick gave a small, rueful smile. "We did."

Alex leaned back slightly. "It makes sense," she said. "Different locations, different conditions, different adjustments."

William shook his head once. "Different expressions of the same pattern."

Fredrick let that sit for a moment. He had heard versions of that thought over the past two weeks, but it still carried weight each time it was spoken. "Go on," he said.

William gestured toward the map. "The interference isn't random. It's consistent within context. Low terrain accumulates density. Density affects signal propagation. Each site tried to compensate locally instead of aligning with the broader pattern."

Alex nodded. "So every site was correcting for symptoms, not cause."

"Yes."

Fredrick looked at the display again, this time with a different kind of focus. "Which means if we had recognized the pattern earlier…"

"You would have adjusted the network differently from the beginning," William said.

Fredrick gave a short breath that might have been a laugh if it had carried more humor. "That would have saved us a great deal of time."

"It also would have required a different way of looking at the problem," William said.

Alex glanced at him. "Which most people don't do under pressure."

William did not answer that. He didn't need to.

The shuttle banked slightly to the east, bringing another section of the planet into view. This region was more broken than the one they had just left. The ridges were steeper, the gaps between them deeper, and in several places the land seemed to drop away into narrow cuts that disappeared into shadow even under full daylight.

Alex studied one of those formations as it passed beneath them. "That looks like a canyon system," she said.

Fredrick leaned forward again. "It is. Runs for several kilometers. Narrow in places. Hard to navigate on the ground."

William's attention settled there for a moment longer than it had on the other terrain features. From above, the canyon looked like a dark seam cut into the surface, its edges uneven and sharp. Even at this height, there was something about it that suggested confinement—space without openness, movement without freedom.

"Does it affect the network?" Alex asked.

Fredrick nodded. "More than we'd like. Signal drops sharply in those regions. We try to route around them whenever possible."

William's gaze remained on the canyon. "And when you can't?"

Fredrick hesitated. "We lose consistency."

Alex shifted her focus back to the map. "We didn't have a site down there."

"No," Fredrick said. "No one was eager to build one."

William said nothing, but he continued to watch the canyon until the shuttle carried them past it and the land opened again into broader stretches of rock and low vegetation.

The pilot's voice came over the cabin speaker. "We'll be on approach to Outpost Meridian in just under an hour. Conditions are clear at base. Minor wind variance on the western ridge."

"Thank you," Alex said automatically.

Fredrick settled back into his seat and closed his eyes for a moment. "You know," he said after a few seconds, "when we first started having problems with the network, we assumed it was a matter of scale. Too many settlements, too much distance, too much variation. We brought in specialists who knew more about signal amplification than anyone on Meridian. They upgraded hardware, recalibrated systems, replaced components that didn't need replacing. And every time, it worked—for a while."

Alex glanced at him. "Until the environment shifted again."

"Yes."

William folded his hands loosely in front of him. "The system wasn't designed for this planet."

Fredrick opened one eye. "No," he said. "It wasn't."

Alex leaned forward slightly, studying the data again. "But it can be adapted."

"Yes," William said.

Fredrick turned his head and looked at him. "You say that very simply."

"It is simple," William said. "Not easy. But simple."

Fredrick let out a quiet chuckle. "There's a difference."

"Yes."

For a time, none of them spoke.

The shuttle moved steadily across the sky, its engines a low, constant presence beneath the quiet of the cabin. Below them, Virella passed in long, measured stretches—ridge, basin, plateau, and occasional flashes of reflective mineral where the light caught at the right angle.

Alex broke the silence first. "The second site," she said, scrolling through her notes. "The one near the northern rise. That one didn't behave like the others at first."

Fredrick nodded. "No, it didn't."

William looked at her. "The ground composition was different."

"Yes," Alex said. "Higher mineral density. It changed how the signal grounded."

Fredrick smiled faintly. "That was the one where you told me we'd been 'solving the wrong problem in the right place.'"

Alex gave a small shrug. "It fit."

"It did," Fredrick said.

William's expression remained neutral, but there was a quiet acknowledgment in his eyes as he looked between them. These were the moments that mattered to him—not the correction itself, but the understanding that followed. A system that could be explained could be maintained. A problem that could be understood would not need to be solved again the same way.

Alex closed the file and set the tablet aside. "Once Meridian integrates the full adjustment set," she said, "the network should stabilize across all twelve settlements."

Fredrick nodded. "We'll run full-cycle tests over the next several days. Day, dusk, night, and early morning. If the pattern holds—"

"It will," William said.

Fredrick looked at him. "You're certain."

William met his gaze. "Yes."

There was no emphasis in the word. No insistence. Just certainty.

Fredrick held that for a moment, then gave a slow nod. "Then for the first time since we established the outer ring, we'll have a network we can rely on."

Alex leaned back in her seat, her posture relaxing just slightly now that the work was behind them. "That will make everything else easier," she said. "Coordination, supply movement, emergency response."

"Everything," Fredrick agreed.

William turned his attention forward again. In the distance, just visible through the forward glass, a larger structure began to take shape against the horizon. Outpost Meridian.

Even from this distance, it stood apart from the other settlements. Larger, more structured, built not just to survive but to serve as the center point for everything around it. Towers rose from its core, not as tall as the communications mast they had just left, but broader, more stable, designed to carry the load of a system that connected people across a difficult world.

Fredrick followed his gaze. "Home," he said quietly.

Alex smiled faintly. "For now."

William said nothing.

He watched the outpost grow larger as they approached, its form resolving into familiar lines and structures. The network they had just repaired would converge there, every adjusted signal, every corrected relay, every stabilized connection feeding back into the central system.

For the first time since they had arrived on Virella, the Meridian network would function as it had been intended.

That was enough.

For now.

The shuttle continued its steady approach, and the land of Virella stretched beneath them—vast, uneven, and quietly complex, holding more patterns than most people ever saw.

William's gaze shifted once more, briefly, to the deeper terrain they had passed earlier.

The canyon.

Then he looked forward again.

There were always more patterns.

And not all of them revealed themselves in time.

## Chapter 3 - Return to Meridian

Outpost Meridian rose from the stone like something built to endure rather than impress.

From a distance, it appeared almost geometric—clean lines, reinforced angles, a deliberate order imposed on a landscape that resisted it at every turn. As the shuttle descended, that impression gave way to detail. Surface wear along the outer structures. Reinforced plating where earlier designs had proven insufficient. Secondary supports added after the fact, not for symmetry, but because something had once failed and someone had learned from it.

Alex watched the approach with a practiced eye. "Wind's stronger on the western ridge than they reported," she said.

The pilot adjusted slightly. "It's within tolerance."

"It always is," Alex replied.

Fredrick smiled faintly at that. "You'll find Meridian has a habit of reporting conditions just accurately enough to be technically correct."

Alex didn't look away from the forward glass. "That's one way to build confidence."

William stood just behind them, one hand resting lightly against the back of a seat, steady without effort as the shuttle made its final approach. He had already taken in most of what he needed from the descent. The placement of the outer relay structures. The alignment of the central tower. The way the surrounding terrain shaped the airflow and, more subtly, how the light moved across the surface of the outpost as the sun lowered toward evening.

Meridian had been designed well.

It had simply been asked to operate on a world that did not behave the way its designers had expected.

The shuttle touched down with a controlled, measured impact. Not abrupt, not gentle—just precise. Outside, the landing platform was already active. Personnel moved with purpose rather than urgency, equipment carts crossing the pad in predictable paths, a pair of technicians pausing just long enough to glance toward the shuttle before returning to their work.

This was not a place that reacted dramatically.

It adapted.

The hatch opened, and the cooler air of early evening moved through the cabin.

Fredrick was the first to stand. "You'll want to let me speak first," he said, half-turning toward William and Alex. "If I don't, they'll start asking questions before we're halfway down the ramp."

Alex unlatched the field kit. "That sounds familiar."

"It should," Fredrick said. "You've been with me for the last six sites."

"That's how I know," she replied.

William lifted the smaller case without comment and followed them toward the exit.

Outside, a small group had already formed near the base of the ramp. Not a crowd—Meridian didn't gather crowds for routine arrivals—but enough to indicate that this return mattered. At the front stood a man in a dark, reinforced jacket, his posture straight, his expression controlled. Beside him was a woman holding a data slate, her attention already moving between the shuttle, the incoming team, and whatever reports she had queued for review.

Fredrick stepped down onto the platform and gave a short nod. "Director Kessler."

The man inclined his head. "Mercer." His gaze shifted briefly to William and Alex, then back again. "You're back ahead of schedule."

Fredrick gave a small shrug. "The final site didn't require the delay we anticipated."

Kessler's eyes narrowed slightly. "That suggests either the problem was simpler than expected… or your solution was."

Fredrick allowed himself the faintest hint of a smile. "Neither."

That earned a brief pause.

Kessler looked past him. "William Arden."

William stepped forward. "Director."

Kessler studied him for a moment, not with skepticism exactly, but with the careful assessment of someone accustomed to measuring outcomes rather than promises. "We've been receiving stable transmission reports from the outer settlements for the past several hours," he said. "Including the final site."

"Yes," William said.

Kessler's gaze sharpened slightly. "Consistent stability?"

"Yes."

There was no elaboration.

Kessler seemed to consider asking for more, then decided against it. He turned slightly toward the woman beside him. "Log the update," he said. "Full verification cycle begins immediately."

She nodded and made a quick notation.

Alex stepped forward just enough to be included without interrupting. "You'll want to run the cycle across multiple intervals," she said. "Day, dusk, night, and early morning. The pattern should hold, but confirmation matters."

The woman glanced up, assessing, then nodded again. "Understood."

Kessler's attention returned to Alex briefly, then to Fredrick. "You brought the right team," he said.

Fredrick did not look at William or Alex. "Yes," he said simply.

There was a brief silence, not uncomfortable, just transitional.

Then Kessler stepped back. "We'll debrief in one hour," he said. "You'll want time to settle in first."

Fredrick inclined his head. "Appreciated."

Kessler turned and walked away without further comment, the woman falling into step beside him, already reviewing data.

Alex watched them go, then looked at Fredrick. "He doesn't waste time."

"No," Fredrick said. "He doesn't."

William stepped aside to allow a transport cart to pass, then looked across the platform. Meridian was exactly as he remembered it—efficient, structured, and built with a kind of quiet determination that matched the people who lived and worked there.

"Let's get the equipment secured," Alex said. "Then we can organize the reports before the debrief."

Fredrick gave a small, approving nod. "You've been doing this long enough that I don't need to remind you of anything."

Alex glanced at him. "You still do."

Fredrick smiled. "Yes. I suppose I do."

They moved off the platform together, passing into the main corridor that led toward the central operations wing.

Inside, Meridian felt different than the outer settlements. The structures were larger, the corridors wider, the systems more integrated. Screens displayed network status across multiple sectors. Personnel moved with purpose, but without the edge of strain William had seen elsewhere. Here, the system had always functioned—if not perfectly, then well enough to maintain order.

Now, it would do better than that.

As they walked, Alex adjusted her pace slightly to match William's. "We should consolidate the adjustment logs before the debrief," she said. "If they start asking for specifics, it'll be easier if everything is already structured."

"It is," William said.

Alex gave him a brief look. "In your head, yes. Not necessarily for everyone else."

"That's why you're here," he said.

She accepted that without comment.

Fredrick glanced back at them. "I heard that."

Alex didn't miss a step. "You were meant to."

They reached the equipment bay and set their cases down along a marked station. Alex immediately began organizing the contents—tools separated, data modules aligned, notes transferred into a cleaner format. William watched for a moment, then turned his attention to the network display mounted on the far wall.

All twelve settlements were visible.

Each one showed a stable connection.

The lines between them—once inconsistent, flickering, unreliable—now held steady.

Fredrick came to stand beside him. "It's been a long time since I've seen it look like that," he said quietly.

William nodded once.

Fredrick folded his arms loosely. "Do you ever get used to it?"

"To what?"

"Fixing something that everyone else has been struggling with for months."

William considered that for a moment. "No."

Fredrick glanced at him. "No?"

"No," William said. "Because the problem is different each time."

Fredrick smiled faintly. "That's one way to look at it."

Alex closed the final case and stepped over to join them. "We should head to the briefing room," she said. "They won't wait long."

Fredrick straightened. "No. They won't."

They moved through the corridor toward the central briefing area, passing several personnel who paused just long enough to acknowledge Fredrick before continuing on their way. A few glanced at William, recognition beginning to spread in small, quiet ways. Nothing dramatic. Just awareness.

Inside the briefing room, Director Kessler was already seated at the far end of the table. The woman from the landing platform stood beside a display panel, data already arranged in layered sequences.

"Let's begin," Kessler said as they entered.

The next hour passed with efficiency.

Fredrick outlined the original problem. Alex presented the structured adjustments. William clarified only where necessary, focusing on underlying patterns rather than surface-level corrections. Questions were asked. Answers were given. Data was reviewed. Assumptions were corrected.

At no point did the discussion become heated.

Meridian did not operate that way.

When it was finished, Kessler leaned back slightly in his chair and regarded them with the same measured expression he had worn since the beginning.

"The network will hold," he said.

"Yes," William replied.

Kessler nodded once. "Then we move forward."

It was not praise.

It was acceptance.

The meeting ended without ceremony.

As they stepped back into the corridor, the sense of completion settled in more fully. The work was done. The network was stable. The settlements were connected.

Fredrick exhaled slowly as they walked. "I think that's the first time in months I've walked out of that room without a list of unresolved issues."

Alex smiled faintly. "Enjoy it."

"I intend to," he said.

They reached the outer section of the facility, where the evening light filtered in through reinforced panels. The sky above Virella had shifted again, the color deepening as the sun moved lower, the distant ridges fading into softer tones.

For a moment, none of them spoke.

Then Fredrick looked toward the transit schedule display. "The return shuttle leaves in the morning," he said. "We'll be back at the Meridian hub within two days."

Alex nodded. "That's sooner than I expected."

"So did I," Fredrick said. "I was prepared to be here another week."

William looked out toward the horizon.

"Everything is working," Fredrick continued. "The network is stable. The settlements are connected. For the first time since we built the outer ring, Meridian isn't compensating for failure."

He turned slightly toward William. "You did what we needed."

William did not respond immediately.

He was watching the distant terrain again, the way the light settled unevenly across the surface, the way the lower regions seemed to gather shadow just a little earlier than the rest.

Patterns.

There were always patterns.

Alex noticed the direction of his attention. "What is it?" she asked.

William shifted his gaze back to the outpost. "Nothing," he said.

Fredrick studied him for a moment, then nodded once, as if deciding not to press further. "Well," he said, "for now, I suggest we take advantage of the fact that everything is working and get some rest."

Alex agreed. "That sounds like a good plan."

William inclined his head slightly.

They turned back toward the interior of Outpost Meridian, the steady hum of the functioning network surrounding them, every connection holding as it should.

For the first time since they had arrived on Virella, there was nothing left to fix.

At least, that was how it appeared.

Morning would come soon enough.

And with it, the journey home.

## Chapter 4 - In Transit

Morning on Virella arrived without softness.

The light came clean and direct across the ridges, cutting long lines through the thinner air above Outpost Meridian. There was no gradual warming, no gentle transition from dark to day. The night simply gave way, and the world resumed.

By the time William and Alex reached the landing platform, the shuttle was already in final preparation.

Ground crews moved with quiet efficiency around the craft, checking seals, verifying load balance, and confirming flight clearance. A light wind crossed the platform from the eastern rise, carrying with it the dry, mineral scent that seemed to define the planet itself.

Fredrick Mercer was already there.

He stood near the base of the ramp speaking with one of the crew, his posture relaxed in a way William had not seen since their arrival on Virella. There was something lighter in him now—not carelessness, but the easing of a burden that had been carried longer than it should have been.

He glanced up as William and Alex approached. "Good timing," he said. "We're just about ready to board."

Alex adjusted the strap of her field kit. "Passenger count confirmed?"

Fredrick nodded. "Twenty-five total. Crew, returning personnel, and a few transfers heading back through Meridian before moving on."

Alex gave a small, approving nod. "That's manageable."

Fredrick smiled faintly. "That's exactly what I said."

William's attention shifted toward the shuttle. The hatch was open, and movement inside suggested that boarding had already begun. He watched for a moment, not focusing on any one person, but taking in the pattern of motion—the way people entered, where they paused, how they arranged themselves once inside.

Then he stepped forward.

The interior of the shuttle was arranged in two parallel rows of seats with a central aisle, functional and efficient. There was no attempt at comfort beyond what was necessary. This was a working transport, not a passenger vessel designed for long-distance travel.

Alex moved down the aisle first, scanning quickly, noting faces, positions, spacing. William followed more slowly.

Fredrick came in behind them.

"Take seats where you like," he said. "We've got enough room that no one needs to crowd."

That proved mostly true.

The first few rows were already occupied by crew-adjacent personnel—technicians and support staff who were accustomed to travel and settled quickly without drawing attention. Farther back, a small cluster of individuals sat together, their posture more guarded, their attention less outward. Two uniformed guards occupied seats on either side of them, not overtly restrictive, but clearly positioned with purpose.

Alex glanced briefly in that direction.

"Prisoner transfer?" she asked quietly.

Fredrick nodded. "Four of them. Being moved through Meridian to a holding facility off-world."

Alex studied them for a moment longer, then nodded once and moved on.

William paused just slightly as his gaze passed over the group.

One of the prisoners met his eyes.

He was younger than the others—late twenties perhaps—with a stillness about him that did not match the rest of the group. Where the others shifted, watched, measured their surroundings, this one simply observed. Not tense. Not relaxed. Just… present.

William held the look for a fraction of a second, then moved on.

Alex had taken a seat midway down the cabin, leaving the adjacent place open without comment. William sat beside her, setting his case at his feet.

Fredrick took the aisle seat across from them.

"Good positioning," he said quietly.

Alex glanced at him. "Habit."

Fredrick nodded. "Useful one."

Boarding continued.

A man in his mid-thirties with a confident, almost practiced ease took a seat two rows ahead on the opposite side. He greeted one of the crew by name, exchanged a few light words, and then settled in with the look of someone accustomed to being comfortable in most environments.

Alex leaned slightly toward William. "That one's used to leading," she said under her breath.

William followed her glance. "Yes."

"Doesn't mean he should be," she added.

William said nothing.

Across the aisle, one of the guards adjusted his position slightly, not in response to anything specific, but in quiet awareness. The prisoners remained seated. One leaned back with a look of open disinterest. Another watched the cabin with the careful attention of someone measuring distance and opportunity. The younger one—the one who had met William's gaze—looked down at his hands, then up again, taking in the room without expression.

Fredrick followed William's line of sight. "Darren Kroll," he said quietly. "Technical background. Not where he should have ended up."

William nodded once.

"Most of them aren't," Fredrick added.

Alex glanced across the aisle. "Some are."

Fredrick gave a small, noncommittal sound. "Perhaps."

The hatch closed with a firm, sealed tone.

A moment later, the pilot's voice came over the cabin system. "All passengers secure. Departure in thirty seconds. Estimated transit to outbound relay: one hour."

The shuttle lifted smoothly from the platform.

Through the side window, Outpost Meridian fell away beneath them, its structured lines shrinking against the broader sweep of Virella's terrain. The central tower stood clear against the morning sky, its signal now stable, its connections holding across all twelve settlements.

For a moment, William watched it.

Then he turned his attention forward.

The shuttle climbed steadily, banking slightly as it aligned with its outbound path. Below, the land opened again into the now-familiar pattern of ridges, basins, and long, uneven stretches of rock and mineral soil.

The flight settled into routine.

At first.

Conversation began in low tones throughout the cabin. Nothing loud. Nothing disruptive. Just the quiet exchange of people returning from work completed or transitioning toward whatever came next.

Fredrick spoke briefly with one of the crew across the aisle, confirming final reports and transmission logs. Alex reviewed her notes one last time, then set them aside, her posture easing slightly now that there was nothing left to organize.

William sat still.

Not inactive. Just… still.

His attention moved through the cabin without obvious focus, noting the rhythm of conversation, the placement of individuals, the subtle tensions that existed without being spoken.

Two rows ahead, the confident man Alex had noted earlier shifted in his seat and turned slightly, his voice carrying just enough to be heard without being directed.

"You're the one who fixed the outer sites," he said.

It was not quite a question.

William looked up. "We made adjustments."

The man smiled faintly. "That's one way to describe it. I've been hearing about it since yesterday."

Fredrick leaned forward slightly. "Gideon Trask," he said, by way of introduction.

"William Arden," Gideon replied, though it was clear he already knew.

Alex gave a brief nod. "Alex Hale."

Gideon inclined his head in return. "Impressive work."

William did not respond immediately.

Then, simply: "It needed to be done."

Gideon's smile remained, but something in his expression shifted—not challenged, exactly, but engaged. "Most things do," he said. "The question is usually how."

Alex glanced between them, then leaned back slightly in her seat.

Fredrick watched the exchange with quiet interest.

Across the aisle, one of the prisoners—Silas Venn—snorted softly, just loud enough to be heard. "All this talk about fixing things," he muttered. "Let's see how well it holds."

One of the guards shifted. "Keep it down."

Silas leaned back, unbothered.

Darren Kroll said nothing.

Tarin Jex, seated beside him, tilted his head slightly, watching the interaction with mild curiosity.

The shuttle continued its steady climb.

For several minutes, nothing changed.

Then—

A flicker.

So slight it might have been missed.

One of the forward panels blinked once, the display shifting out of alignment for less than a second before correcting itself.

Alex saw it.

Her posture changed immediately—not dramatically, but enough.

"Did you see that?" she asked quietly.

Fredrick turned. "See what?"

William's gaze had already moved to the panel.

"Yes," he said.

Another flicker.

Longer this time.

The pilot's voice came over the system, calm but more focused than before. "Minor instrumentation fluctuation. Stand by."

Alex didn't look away from the display. "That's not random."

"No," William said.

Gideon turned slightly in his seat. "Something wrong?"

Fredrick was already watching the panel. "It shouldn't be," he said.

A low distortion crackled briefly through the cabin speakers—too short to be a full signal interruption, too irregular to be standard interference.

William's attention shifted, not to the panel, but to the space beyond the window.

Below them, the terrain had changed again.

The shuttle was crossing over a region of deeper cuts and shadowed lines—terrain that dropped away more sharply than the surrounding ridges.

The canyon.

Alex followed his gaze. "We're over the low region."

Fredrick leaned forward. "That shouldn't affect—"

The panel flickered again.

This time, it did not correct immediately.

The line of data across the display fractured into overlapping segments, each slightly out of sync with the others.

The pilot's voice returned. "We're reading inconsistent instrument feedback. Attempting recalibration."

The cabin grew quieter.

Not silent.

Just… attentive.

William watched the terrain below, then the panel, then the subtle change in the air inside the shuttle—not physical, but perceptual. A shift in expectation. A recognition that something was not behaving the way it should.

He did not move.

He did not speak immediately.

He observed.

Alex glanced at him. "This is the same pattern."

"Yes."

Fredrick looked between them. "You're saying this is the same interference we were just correcting?"

William shook his head slightly. "Not the same."

"Then what?"

William's eyes remained on the display.

"A different expression of it."

The panel flickered again.

This time, longer.

And the line did not settle cleanly when it returned.

The pilot's voice came back, more controlled now. "We're seeing signal distortion across multiple systems. Beginning full diagnostic."

Gideon leaned back slightly, his earlier ease replaced by a sharper focus. "That doesn't sound minor."

"No," Alex said quietly.

Across the aisle, even Silas had gone still.

Darren Kroll's gaze had lifted again, not to the panel this time, but to William.

Watching.

Measuring.

Waiting.

William remained seated, his expression unchanged.

But his attention had narrowed.

The pattern was there.

It was just not yet fully visible.

The shuttle continued forward, carrying them deeper across the broken terrain of Virella.

And something—something in the system, or in the environment, or in the interaction between the two—

was beginning to come apart.

## Chapter 5 - The Incident

The flicker did not stop.

It settled, for a moment, into something that almost looked stable—but it wasn't. The display ahead of the cabin held its lines, then shifted just slightly out of alignment, as though two versions of the same data were trying to occupy the same space.

William watched it without speaking.

Alex didn't look away. "It's not random," she said again, quieter now.

"No," William said.

Fredrick leaned forward in his seat, eyes fixed on the forward panel. "We're above the canyon," he said. "But that shouldn't—"

The cabin speakers crackled.

Not loudly. Not violently. Just enough to interrupt the rhythm of the space.

"—control feedback unstable," the pilot's voice cut in and out, then returned. "Recalibrating primary systems. Stand by."

The shuttle continued forward.

But something had changed.

It wasn't the motion. Not yet. It was the sense of alignment—the quiet, unnoticed agreement between system and environment that allowed everything to function without thought. That agreement was slipping.

Alex shifted slightly in her seat. "William."

He nodded once.

"I see it."

Across the aisle, Gideon Trask leaned forward just enough to look toward the forward instruments. "You want to tell the rest of us what you're seeing?"

William didn't answer immediately.

He watched the panel again as it flickered—this time not in a single line, but across multiple systems. Navigation, environmental readings, signal alignment. Each one lagged behind the others by a fraction of a second, then corrected, then slipped again.

Not failure.

Misalignment.

Fredrick followed his gaze. "It's the same pattern," he said. "The same kind of distortion we were correcting at the sites."

"Yes," William said.

"Then why is it happening here?"

William's eyes moved briefly to the window, to the terrain below, then back again.

"Because here," he said, "the system is moving through it."

Fredrick opened his mouth to respond—

The shuttle lurched.

Not sharply. Not enough to throw anyone from their seat. But enough that every conversation in the cabin stopped at once.

The pilot's voice came back, tighter now. "We're experiencing instability in flight control feedback. Attempting manual override."

Alex's hand moved to the edge of the console in front of her, steadying without tension. "That's not just signal," she said. "That's control response."

"Yes."

The panel flickered again.

Longer.

This time, when it returned, the horizon line on the forward display was off by several degrees.

Then it corrected.

Then it slipped again.

Fredrick's voice dropped. "That's not possible."

"It is," William said.

"How?"

William didn't answer right away.

He watched the delay.

Measured it.

Felt it.

"Because the system isn't receiving consistent positional data," he said. "It's reacting to interference before it can reconcile it."

Gideon's voice cut in, sharper now. "Then fix it."

William turned his head slightly. "We're not in control of it."

Another lurch.

Stronger.

This time a few people grabbed for the edges of their seats.

From the back of the cabin, one of the prisoners—Tarin—let out a low whistle. "That doesn't feel like routine turbulence."

"No," Alex said.

The pilot's voice again, no longer attempting calm beyond what was necessary. "Control systems are not responding consistently. Switching to full manual."

A second voice—co-pilot—came in underneath. "Manual input lagging. We're getting delayed response."

Fredrick's hand tightened on the armrest. "Delayed?"

"Yes," William said quietly. "The system is responding to where it thinks we are… not where we are."

The cabin fell still.

That was worse than failure.

Failure could be corrected.

This—

This meant the system could not be trusted.

The shuttle dipped.

Not a drop.

A shift.

The kind that suggested the correction had come too late.

Alex leaned forward slightly. "They're compensating after the fact."

"Yes."

Another flicker.

This time, the lights themselves dimmed briefly before returning.

The sound changed.

Subtle—but unmistakable.

The engines were no longer in perfect harmony.

Fredrick looked at William. "Can they stabilize it?"

William watched the panel again.

The delay had increased.

The misalignment was widening.

"No," he said.

That word settled into the cabin like weight.

Gideon straightened. "Then what are they doing?"

William's voice remained level. "Trying to maintain control long enough to land."

"Land where?" someone behind them asked.

No one answered.

The pilot did.

"Emergency descent," he said over the system. "All passengers remain seated. Secure positions immediately."

The shuttle tilted.

This time there was no mistaking it.

They were descending.

Fast.

Alex's voice stayed steady. "William."

"I know."

She didn't ask anything else.

Across the aisle, the guards had shifted, their attention no longer on the prisoners but on the cabin itself. Silas Venn had braced his feet against the deck, a grin that wasn't humor pulling slightly at one side of his mouth.

"Now this," he said quietly, "is interesting."

Darren Kroll didn't move.

He watched.

The shuttle dropped again.

Harder.

The canyon walls rose into view through the forward glass—too close, too fast, the narrow cut of terrain revealing itself in sharp, uneven lines.

Fredrick's voice was low. "They're not going to clear that."

"They're not trying to," William said.

The pilot's voice again. "We're taking it down inside the canyon. Brace for impact."

The word hung in the air.

Impact.

Alex's hand moved, not in panic, but with purpose—checking the restraint across her shoulder, adjusting the positioning of the equipment case at her feet so it wouldn't shift into the aisle.

William did the same.

Not hurried.

Precise.

The shuttle banked sharply.

The canyon walls filled the view—stone rising on both sides, the space between them narrower than it had appeared from above.

The engines surged.

Then adjusted.

Then surged again.

Each correction a fraction too late.

Fredrick closed his eyes briefly, then opened them again. "Well," he said quietly, "this isn't how I planned to end the trip."

Alex didn't look at him. "Then we'll plan the next part."

Another drop.

Closer now.

The ground rushed up—not flat, not smooth, but broken, uneven, unforgiving.

The pilot's voice, controlled through force of will. "Final approach. Brace."

William's gaze fixed forward.

Not on the ground.

On the pattern.

On the timing.

On the way the system lagged behind reality by just enough to make every correction late.

There was no time to change it.

Only time to endure it.

The shuttle hit.

Not with a single catastrophic impact—but with a sequence.

First contact—

A violent jolt as the landing struts struck uneven ground.

A skid—

The hull scraping, twisting, metal protesting against stone.

A second impact—

Harder.

The left side dipping, then slamming back as the pilot fought to keep the craft upright.

Something tore free somewhere behind them.

A shout—

Cut short.

The shuttle slid—

Then struck again.

And stopped.

The sound ended.

Not gradually.

All at once.

Silence.

For a moment, nothing moved.

No one spoke.

The world held itself in place as if deciding whether it would continue.

Then—

A low creak.

Metal settling.

Air shifting.

Alex was the first to move.

Not quickly.

Deliberately.

"William," she said.

"I'm here."

Fredrick drew in a slow breath. "That," he said quietly, "was not ideal."

Alex reached for the release on her restraint. "Everyone stay where you are," she called, her voice steady and clear despite the ringing quiet around them. "Give it a moment."

A few people shifted anyway.

Someone in the back groaned.

The smell reached them next.

Not fire.

Not yet.

But heat.

Stressed systems.

Possibility.

William unlatched his restraint and stood carefully, testing balance before committing weight.

The shuttle held.

For now.

He looked toward the front of the cabin.

The forward panel was dark.

Not flickering.

Not misaligned.

Just—

Off.

Outside the forward glass, the canyon walls rose high on both sides, the sky above them a narrow strip of pale blue.

They were down.

Inside.

Contained.

Alex moved into the aisle. "If you're injured, say so now. If you're not, stay seated until we clear the exits."

Her voice carried.

It gave shape to the moment.

Fredrick pushed himself upright more slowly. "I'll assist," he said.

William nodded once.

Behind them, Darren Kroll was already watching the interior of the shuttle, his eyes moving over damage, structure, possibility.

Silas Venn leaned forward, testing his footing. "Well," he said under his breath, "we're not flying anymore."

No one answered him.

Because now—

Now the real problem had begun.

## Chapter 6 - First Minutes

For a few seconds after the impact, no one moved.

It wasn't hesitation.

It was instinct.

The kind that told you not to trust the stillness right after something had gone wrong.

The shuttle creaked again—metal adjusting under stress, weight redistributing across a structure that had not been designed to sit at this angle. A faint hiss came from somewhere toward the rear, steady but not escalating.

Alex stood in the aisle, one hand braced lightly against the seatback beside her, her eyes already moving from person to person.

"Listen carefully," she said, her voice clear and controlled. "If you can move, stay where you are for the next ten seconds. Let the structure settle. If you're hurt, tell me now."

A man near the front raised his hand slightly. "Shoulder," he said through clenched teeth.

"Stay seated," Alex replied. "We'll get to you."

Another voice from the back. "I'm—" It cut off into a sharp breath. "Leg. I think it's broken."

"Don't move it," Alex said immediately. "Stay still."

William moved forward, one step at a time, testing each shift in weight before committing. The deck was angled slightly, not enough to make standing impossible, but enough to change how force moved through the structure. He glanced toward the forward section.

The pilot and co-pilot were still in their seats.

Conscious.

The pilot was already reaching for the manual override panel.

"Systems are down," he said without turning. "Power's not responding."

William looked once at the forward display—dark, unresponsive—then shifted his attention to the structure around them.

"Is there fire risk?" he asked.

The co-pilot shook his head slightly. "Not immediate. We shut down before full failure. Fuel lines should be intact—but I wouldn't bet on that holding if something shifts."

William nodded once. "Then we move quickly."

Alex was already unfastening the first injured passenger's restraint. "If you're not hurt," she said, raising her voice just enough to carry through the cabin, "you're going to help the person next to you. We move out in pairs. No one rushes. No one pushes."

Fredrick moved into the aisle, steady at first—then paused briefly, one hand pressing lightly against his side before continuing.

It was small enough that no one commented on it.

He didn't either.

He rested one hand briefly against a seat as he found his balance. "You heard her," he said. "Follow instructions. We'll all get out faster that way."

There was something about the tone—steady, familiar—that settled the edges of rising panic before it could take hold.

Across the aisle, one of the guards had already released his harness and turned toward the prisoners. "Stay seated," he said.

Silas Venn gave a short, humorless laugh. "Not planning on running," he said. "Where would I go?"

The guard didn't answer.

Darren Kroll was already unfastening his restraint, his movements controlled, precise. He stood carefully, testing the tilt of the floor, then reached down and steadied the man beside him before the guard could intervene.

The guard hesitated.

Then allowed it.

Tarin Jex rose more slowly, his eyes moving over the cabin, measuring, assessing. "Well," he murmured, "this just became a very different kind of trip."

Alex didn't look at him. "If you can stand, you can carry," she said. "Find someone who can't."

Tarin paused for a fraction of a second, then gave a small nod. "Fair enough."

William moved toward the rear of the cabin, where the hiss was coming from.

It wasn't loud.

Not yet.

But it was steady.

A panel along the lower wall had buckled slightly inward, and a thin line of vapor leaked through a seam that should not have been open.

He crouched, studying it.

Pressure release.

Not explosive.

But not safe either.

"Rear section compromised," he said. "We need to clear this area first."

Alex nodded without looking up. "Then we start from the back."

She turned, scanning quickly. "You—" she pointed to a man who was already standing. "Take him." She nodded toward the injured passenger with the leg injury. "Support under the arm. Do not move the leg."

Fredrick stepped in beside them. "I'll take the other side."

The man nodded, and together they began easing the injured passenger out of his seat.

A low groan escaped him as they lifted.

"Easy," Alex said. "Slow. Let him set the pace."

William stood and moved back toward the center of the cabin. "Exit?" he asked the pilot.

"Rear hatch should still function," the pilot said. "Manual release."

William nodded once and turned.

The hatch control panel was intact, though the indicator lights were dead. He placed his hand on the manual override and pulled.

For a moment, nothing happened.

Then—

A heavy mechanical release.

The hatch shifted.

Opened.

Cool air rushed in from outside, carrying the scent of stone and something faintly metallic.

The canyon.

William stepped aside. "We have an exit," he said.

Alex didn't look up. "Then we move."

One by one, they began guiding people toward the rear.

Not quickly.

Not chaotically.

Deliberately.

The injured first.

Then those who could assist.

Then the rest.

Outside, the ground was uneven, broken stone and loose debris scattered around the hull where the shuttle had struck and slid to a stop. The craft rested at a slight angle, its left side lower than the right, one of the landing struts partially collapsed beneath it.

Fredrick stepped down first with the injured passenger, testing the ground before shifting full weight. "Stable enough," he called up.

Alex followed, then turned immediately to receive the next person.

"Keep them moving away from the hull," she said. "We don't know how stable it is."

William remained inside until the last of the rear passengers had cleared, his attention moving constantly—structure, movement, sound.

Across the aisle, one of the guards hesitated, glancing at the prisoners.

Silas met his gaze. "You want to go first?" he said. "Be my guest."

The guard shook his head once. "Move."

Silas rose, stepped into the aisle, and moved toward the exit without further comment.

Tarin followed, pausing just long enough to steady another passenger before continuing.

Darren came last among them.

As he reached the hatch, he glanced once at the damaged panel near the rear wall, then at William.

"Pressure line?" he said quietly.

William nodded. "Yes."

Darren looked at it again, measuring something in his head, then stepped down out of the shuttle without another word.

William followed.

Outside, the scale of the canyon became clear.

The walls rose on both sides, steep and uneven, the rock dark and layered, cutting off most of the horizon. The sky above was visible only as a narrow band, pale and distant. The air felt different here—cooler, heavier somehow, as though it lingered longer than it should.

Alex had already begun organizing.

"Medical here," she said, indicating a relatively flat section of ground a short distance from the shuttle. "Keep the injured together. If you can walk, move farther out. We need space."

Fredrick helped lower the injured passenger carefully. "You're doing fine," he said. "Stay with us."

The man nodded, jaw tight.

William stepped back from the group, turning once to take in the full scene.

The shuttle.

The survivors.

The terrain.

Count.

He moved his lips slightly, not speaking aloud.

Then he stepped forward again.

"How many?" Alex asked.

"Twenty-five onboard," Fredrick said. "We need to confirm."

Alex nodded. "We count now."

They moved through the group, not hurried, but efficient.

One by one.

Name.

Response.

Condition.

When they finished, Alex looked up.

"Twenty-five," she said.

William nodded once.

"All accounted for," Fredrick added, relief evident in his voice.

"For now," Alex said quietly.

William turned his gaze back toward the shuttle.

It sat in the canyon like something that did not belong there.

Still.

Damaged.

Uncertain.

The hiss from the rear had not stopped.

The air carried it.

Soft.

Persistent.

A reminder.

They were out.

But they were not safe.

Not yet.

Alex stood, brushing her hands lightly against her sides as she looked over the group. "We stabilize here," she said. "No one goes back inside unless we clear it first."

William nodded.

Fredrick exhaled slowly. "Well," he said, looking up at the narrow strip of sky above them, "we're going to need a new plan."

William followed his gaze.

The canyon walls rose high on either side, cutting them off from distance, from visibility, from anything beyond the immediate space they occupied.

Contained.

"Yes," William said.

"We are."

## Chapter 7 – Triage

The first ten minutes were about movement.

The next ten were about truth.

Alex knelt beside the injured man with the broken leg, her hands already working with calm precision. "Stay with me," she said. "Don't try to help. Just breathe."

He nodded, jaw tight, eyes fixed somewhere beyond her shoulder.

Fredrick hovered nearby, then caught himself and stepped back half a pace—his breath catching slightly as one hand pressed, just briefly, against his side before he let it fall.

It was subtle. Easy to miss.

"What do you need?" he asked.

"Flat support," Alex said. "Something rigid. And I'll need two people to help hold him steady."

"I've got it," Fredrick said, turning immediately. "You—come here." He motioned to two of the standing passengers. "Careful hands. Do exactly what she says."

They moved in, unsure but willing.

Alex didn't look up. "On my count," she said. "We're not setting the bone here, just stabilizing it. If it shifts, it gets worse. Understood?"

Both nodded.

William stepped back from the immediate circle, not out of disinterest, but to see more.

The group had settled into clusters.

Some standing.

Some seated.

Some already helping.

A few simply watching, still caught between what had happened and what it meant.

He began counting again.

Not numbers this time.

Conditions.

Movement.

Capability.

Across the group, Alex's voice continued—steady, controlled, giving shape to what needed to happen next.

"We'll move the critical cases here," she said, indicating a section of ground slightly elevated from the rest. "Keep them off the loose rock. I want clear space around them."

A woman near the front spoke up. "I have basic medical training."

Alex glanced at her. "Good. You're with me. Name?"

"Lena."

"Lena, check for head injuries. Anyone who was thrown forward—start there."

Lena nodded and moved.

Fredrick returned with a panel salvaged from the shuttle's interior. "Will this do?"

Alex looked up briefly. "Yes. That's perfect."

They eased the injured man's leg onto the makeshift support. He cried out once—sharp, involuntary—then clenched his jaw again.

"Easy," Alex said. "You're doing fine."

William shifted his attention to the next cluster.

The man with the shoulder injury.

A woman seated beside him, pressing cloth against a cut along his arm.

Two others standing uncertainly, waiting to be told what to do.

"You're able to move?" William asked the man.

"Yeah," he said, though his voice said otherwise.

William nodded once. "Then sit back. Let them work."

The man hesitated, then did as instructed.

William moved on.

At the edge of the group, one of the guards was speaking quietly with the other, both keeping an eye on the four prisoners without making it the center of attention.

Silas Venn stood with his arms loosely crossed, scanning the canyon with open curiosity. "Not much of a view," he said.

"No," Tarin Jex replied. "But plenty of detail."

Darren Kroll stood a few steps apart from them, his gaze not on the canyon, but on the shuttle.

Studying it.

William followed his line of sight.

The damage was clearer now.

The left landing strut had collapsed almost entirely, forcing the hull into a slight tilt. The underside plating had scraped along the rock during the skid, leaving exposed sections that should not have been visible. The rear panel—where the hiss had begun—showed a warped seam, not torn open, but stressed.

Darren spoke without turning. "If that line gives, it won't explode," he said quietly. "But it'll vent fast."

William stepped closer. "Yes."

Darren glanced at him. "We should move people farther out."

"We will," William said.

Darren nodded once, then returned his attention to the shuttle.

There was no challenge in him.

No attempt to assert.

Just observation.

William turned back toward the group.

"Everyone," he said, raising his voice just enough to carry, "we're moving ten meters farther from the shuttle."

There was a brief pause.

Then Alex looked up. "Do it," she said. "Medical first, then everyone else."

That was enough.

The group shifted.

Carefully.

Those assisting the injured adjusted their grips.

Fredrick moved to help guide the relocation, his voice steady, familiar. "This way. Keep it level. Watch your footing."

Silas stepped aside to clear space without being asked.

Tarin moved ahead, scanning the ground and pointing out more stable footing. "There," he said. "That's better."

Darren remained where he was until the last of the injured had been moved, then followed, his attention still divided between the group and the shuttle.

Once they were clear, Alex stood and looked over the repositioned cluster.

"Good," she said. "That gives us room."

She turned to William. "We need to sort by priority."

He nodded. "Critical. Stable. Functional."

Alex gave the faintest hint of a smile. "Exactly."

They moved together through the group again, this time assigning.

Not formally.

But clearly.

Critical:

The man with the broken leg.

Two others with internal injuries—breathing shallow, color wrong.

Fredrick paused when he saw one of them. "That's Jonas," he said quietly. "He was fine before the descent."

Alex knelt beside Jonas, her expression tightening slightly as she checked his pulse. "He's not now," she said. "Stay with me," she added to him.

Jonas tried to respond.

Didn't quite manage it.

Stable:

The shoulder injury.

Several cuts.

Bruising.

Shock.

Functional:

The rest.

Including—

Alex looked toward the prisoners.

"All of you," she said, "if you can stand and carry, you're working."

Silas raised an eyebrow. "Didn't think we were on the team."

"You are now," Alex said.

Tarin gave a small shrug. "Fair enough."

Darren nodded once.

No one argued.

The guard nearest them looked at Alex, then at William.

William said nothing.

That was enough.

The guard stepped back half a pace.

Roles shifted.

Not announced.

But real.

Fredrick moved between groups, checking, assisting, translating Alex's instructions when needed, steadying those who were beginning to feel the weight of what had happened.

"Stay focused," he said to one man whose hands had begun to shake. "One step at a time. We've got this."

The man nodded, breathing uneven but controlled.

Time passed.

Not long.

But enough.

Then—

Alex's voice changed.

Not louder.

Not sharper.

Just… different.

"William."

He was already turning.

Jonas.

His breathing had become shallow.

Too shallow.

Alex pressed her hand gently against his chest, then checked again. "Jonas," she said. "Stay with me."

There was no response.

Fredrick stepped closer. "What is it?"

Alex didn't answer right away.

She tried again.

Measured.

Precise.

But the pattern wasn't there.

The response wasn't there.

She exhaled slowly.

Then sat back.

Fredrick understood before she spoke.

He looked down at Jonas, then closed his eyes briefly.

Alex's voice was quiet.

"I'm sorry."

No one spoke.

The canyon held the moment.

Not echoing.

Not amplifying.

Just—

Holding it.

Fredrick knelt beside Jonas and rested a hand lightly against his shoulder. "He was one of ours," he said softly. "Good man. Reliable."

Alex bowed her head slightly.

William stood a few steps away, watching.

Not detached.

But still.

He let the moment settle.

Let it take its place.

Then he spoke.

"Alex."

She looked up.

"We continue."

It was not cold.

It was not dismissive.

It was necessary.

Alex held his gaze for a second.

Then nodded.

"Yes," she said.

She rose.

Her voice returned to its earlier steadiness. "We still have critical cases. Stay focused."

The group moved again.

Not with the same uncertainty as before.

Now—

With understanding.

The situation had changed.

Not just survival.

Not just injury.

Loss.

Real.

Immediate.

Fredrick remained where he was for a few seconds longer, then stood and turned back toward the group.

"Let's move," he said.

His voice carried.

And the work continued.

Above them, the narrow strip of sky remained clear.

But along the base of the canyon walls, something faint had begun to gather.

Not visible.

Not yet.

But present.

The air was changing.

And they had only just begun to understand how much that would matter.

## Chapter 8 - Securing the Site

By the time the light began to shift, the group had stopped thinking in terms of the crash.

They were thinking in terms of what came next.

Alex stood near the center of the newly cleared space, hands resting lightly at her sides as she looked over the arrangement they had built in the past hour. It wasn't much. It couldn't be. But it was enough to begin.

The injured were grouped together on the flattest ground they could find, supported by panels and padding pulled from the shuttle. The worst cases had been placed where they could be reached quickly, where Alex and Lena could move between them without stepping over loose rock or navigating unnecessary obstacles.

The rest of the group had settled just beyond them.

Not in neat lines.

Not in formal order.

But close.

Closer than they might have chosen under other circumstances.

William watched that without comment.

People drew together when the environment pressed in.

That was as natural as anything else on Virella.

Fredrick moved through the space with a steady presence, speaking quietly, checking in, making sure that no one had been left without direction. He had always been good at that—seeing what needed to be done before it became obvious.

"Water," he said to one of the men near the edge of the group. "We need to confirm what we have."

"I can check the shuttle," the man said.

William shook his head slightly. "Not yet."

The man hesitated.

"There's still pressure in the rear section," William added. "We don't go back inside until we understand what's stable."

The man nodded. "Right."

Fredrick gave a small approving glance. "We'll inventory once it's safe."

Alex turned toward them. "In the meantime, we ration what we have on hand. If anyone has personal water, bring it forward."

There was a brief pause.

Then, one by one, people stepped forward.

Not all at once.

But enough.

Alex accepted each container, passing them to Lena, who began organizing them into a central supply.

"Good," Alex said. "We'll track it. No one uses anything without checking first."

There were no objections.

Across the space, Tarin Jex crouched near a section of loose stone, testing it with his hand. "This shifts too easily," he said. "If someone steps here in the dark, they're going to lose their footing."

"Then we mark it," Alex said.

Tarin glanced up. "With what?"

William stepped forward, scanning the ground briefly. "Rocks," he said. "Stack them. Build a visible edge."

Tarin nodded once. "That works."

He stood and began gathering stones, placing them in a low, deliberate line that defined the boundary of the safer ground.

Silas Venn watched for a moment, then gave a short breath that might have been a laugh. "So we're building walls now."

"No," Alex said without looking at him. "We're building awareness."

Silas considered that, then shrugged and stepped over to help, moving larger stones into place without further comment.

Darren Kroll remained near the edge of the group, his attention still divided between the shuttle and the surrounding terrain. After a moment, he stepped forward.

"The ground slopes slightly toward the rear of the shuttle," he said. "If anything shifts, that's where it will go."

William nodded. "Then we keep people forward of that line."

Darren pointed. "There. That's the lowest point."

Alex followed his gesture, then turned to Lena. "Mark that as a no-go area. No one crosses it without checking first."

Lena nodded and moved to extend Tarin's boundary markers.

The shape of the camp began to emerge.

Not by design.

By necessity.

A central space for the injured.

A surrounding area for the rest.

Defined edges.

Clear movement paths.

William stepped back again, taking it in.

It wasn't efficient yet.

But it was becoming functional.

Fredrick joined him—slowing just slightly as he approached, one hand resting briefly at his side before he let it fall again.

William noticed.

Fredrick didn't acknowledge it.

"You see it already, don't you?" he said quietly.

William kept his gaze on the group. "Yes."

Fredrick nodded. "Same as the sites."

William glanced at him. "Similar."

Fredrick smiled faintly. "You're going to reorganize it, aren't you?"

"Not yet."

Fredrick folded his arms loosely. "But you will."

William didn't answer.

He didn't need to.

Alex stepped back from the medical area and looked toward the shuttle again. "We need tools," she said. "And more material for support."

William nodded. "We'll take a small team."

Fredrick straightened slightly. "I'll go with you."

Alex shook her head. "No. You stay here."

Fredrick raised an eyebrow. "I'm not injured."

"No," Alex said. "But you're needed here."

There was no argument in her tone.

Just clarity.

Fredrick held her gaze for a moment, then gave a small nod. "All right."

Alex turned to William. "We go in, we take what we need, and we come back out. No extra time."

"Yes."

She looked around. "Two more with us. We need people who can carry and follow instructions."

Darren stepped forward.

"I can help," he said.

Silas followed a half-step behind him. "Might as well," he added.

Alex studied them briefly.

Then nodded. "You stay with us. No one separates."

Neither objected.

Tarin glanced up from his work. "You'll want someone watching the ground," he said. "I'll stay here."

Alex nodded once. "Good."

They moved toward the shuttle.

Up close, the damage felt larger.

More immediate.

The hull bore the marks of impact—scraped metal, bent plating, stress lines that spoke of forces the structure had barely absorbed. The rear section still vented faintly, the hiss quieter now, but present.

William paused at the hatch.

Listened.

Watched.

Then stepped inside.

The interior felt different now.

Not because it had changed.

Because it had stopped working.

The panels were dark.

The systems silent.

Only the structure remained.

Alex moved past him, her focus already on what could be used. "We need med kits, support panels, anything rigid, anything that can carry weight."

Darren moved efficiently, scanning, selecting, lifting.

Silas followed more slowly, but without hesitation, pulling larger pieces free where needed.

William moved toward the rear section, stopping just short of the compromised panel.

The hiss had lessened.

Pressure dropping.

Not stable.

But stabilizing.

"Five minutes," Alex said.

William nodded.

They worked quickly.

Not rushing.

But not wasting motion.

Panels.

Supplies.

Tools.

Each item chosen with purpose.

Then—

A sound.

Not from the rear.

From above.

William's head tilted slightly.

Listening.

Stone.

Shifting.

Very slight.

But real.

He turned toward the hatch. "We're done."

Alex didn't argue. "Move."

They exited the shuttle, carrying what they had gathered.

As they stepped clear, a small cascade of loose rock slipped from the canyon wall above, striking the hull with a series of sharp impacts before settling.

Not a collapse.

A warning.

Silas looked up. "That's comforting."

"No," William said. "It's information."

Silas gave him a look. "Same difference."

"Not at all," William said.

They returned to the group.

Alex immediately began integrating the new supplies into the medical area, reinforcing supports, adjusting positions, improving stability.

Darren set down the panels and stepped back.

Then, without being asked, he moved to the signal unit he had noticed earlier among the salvaged equipment.

He didn't touch it yet.

Just looked.

Measured.

William saw that.

And said nothing.

The light shifted further.

The canyon walls darkened at their base first, shadow rising slowly upward as the sun lowered beyond the ridge.

Fredrick noticed it next.

"The light's changing faster down here," he said.

Alex glanced up. "It's the terrain."

William stepped forward, his attention moving from the group to the edges of the canyon.

The air felt different now.

Heavier.

Not by much.

But enough.

At the base of the walls, something faint had begun to gather.

A softness.

A blurring.

Not yet visible as fog.

But present.

Alex followed his gaze. "It's starting."

William nodded once.

Fredrick looked between them. "What is?"

Alex answered quietly. "The part we haven't dealt with yet."

The group settled in around the newly formed camp.

Boundaries marked.

Supplies gathered.

Injured stabilized—for now.

Above them, the strip of sky narrowed as the light continued to fall.

And along the edges of the canyon floor—

The first trace of fog began to take shape.

Not dramatic.

Not sudden.

But certain.

The day had ended.

And the canyon was beginning to change.

## Chapter 9 - First Night

The fog did not arrive all at once.

It gathered.

At first, it was nothing more than a softening along the base of the canyon walls—a faint loss of detail where stone met shadow. The sharp lines of the rock blurred slightly, as if distance had increased without anything actually moving.

Most of the group did not notice it.

Not immediately.

They were focused on closer things.

On the injured.

On the camp.

On the simple act of settling into a place that had not chosen to receive them.

Alex moved steadily between the medical positions, checking, adjusting, speaking in low, controlled tones. "How's the pain?" she asked one of the injured men.

"Still there," he said through clenched teeth.

"That's expected," she replied. "It's stable. That's what matters."

Lena worked beside her, following instructions without hesitation now, her earlier uncertainty replaced by purpose.

Across the camp, Fredrick Mercer was organizing what remained of their immediate supplies. "Keep everything together," he said, guiding a small cluster of people who had begun to separate items into uneven piles. "We don't have enough to scatter. One place. One record."

Tarin Jex moved along the edge of the marked boundary, adjusting the low line of stones he had helped build earlier. "You'll want to extend this a little farther," he said. "That slope drops off faster than it looks."

Silas Venn stood a few paces behind him, arms loosely folded, watching the canyon with open curiosity. "Still don't see what all the concern is about," he said.

"You will," Tarin replied.

Silas gave a small shrug. "Maybe."

Darren Kroll remained near the center of the camp, close enough to be part of the group, far enough to observe without being drawn into conversation. His attention moved between the people, the shuttle, and the canyon walls—never lingering long in one place, always returning to the same quiet assessment.

William stood just beyond the main cluster, where the marked boundary met the open ground.

He was watching the edges.

Not the camp.

Not the people.

The edges.

The change was clearer now.

The softening at the base of the canyon walls had spread, rising slowly upward, filling the lower contours of the terrain with something that was not quite visible and not quite absent. It moved without motion, present without direction.

Alex stepped up beside him. "It's earlier than I expected," she said.

"Yes."

She crossed her arms lightly, her gaze following his. "It doesn't move like normal fog."

"No."

"What is it?"

William considered that for a moment.

"Accumulation," he said. "Not formation."

Alex frowned slightly. "Meaning?"

"It's not coming in," William said. "It's building where it already is."

She watched it again, then nodded slowly. "Trapped."

"Yes."

Fredrick approached, slowing just slightly as he did, one hand resting briefly against his side before he let it fall again.

"You're both seeing it," he said, his voice steady despite the pause.

"Yes," Alex replied.

Fredrick looked out across the canyon floor. "We've had reports of reduced visibility in low areas before," he said. "But nothing that looked like this."

William's gaze remained steady. "It's the same pattern," he said. "Different scale."

Fredrick let that sit for a moment. "Everything on this planet seems to come back to that."

"Yes."

Behind them, one of the group shifted uneasily. "Is that… fog?" someone asked.

Alex turned slightly. "Yes," she said. "But it's not like what you're used to."

That did not reassure anyone.

The fog continued to rise.

Not quickly.

But steadily.

Within minutes, the lower stones of the boundary line began to fade, their edges softening until they were no longer distinct. The ground itself seemed to lose definition, as if the space between objects had thickened.

"Everyone listen," Alex said, raising her voice just enough to carry. "No one moves beyond the marked line. If you need to step away, you tell someone first. No one goes alone."

There were nods.

Quiet acknowledgments.

The kind that came from understanding rather than argument.

Fredrick added, "We'll set a watch rotation. Two people at a time. We keep eyes on the perimeter."

Silas gave a short breath. "Watch for what?"

"For anything that shouldn't be there," Fredrick said.

Silas looked out into the thickening fog. "That narrows it down."

"It does," Fredrick replied.

Tarin stepped back from the boundary and looked toward William. "You're not just worried about visibility, are you?" he asked.

"No," William said.

Tarin nodded once. "Didn't think so."

The fog reached the first of the outer stones.

Then passed it.

Not over.

Through.

The line did not disappear.

It became harder to see.

Alex watched that carefully. "Markers are only good if you can see them," she said.

William nodded. "We'll need additional reference."

"Sound?" she asked.

"Limited," he said. "Distorted."

Fredrick looked between them. "Distorted how?"

William turned slightly. "Sound will not travel consistently," he said. "Direction will be unreliable."

Fredrick frowned. "You're saying if someone calls out—"

"They may not be where they sound like they are."

Fredrick's expression tightened. "That's not good."

"No."

The fog continued to build.

It reached ankle height.

Then higher.

Not thick enough yet to obscure completely—but enough to alter perception.

The ground seemed farther away than it was.

The space between people less certain.

One of the younger technicians took a step toward the edge of the camp, then stopped, uncertain. "I can't—" he said, then shook his head. "It's closer than it looks."

"Stay where you are," Alex said.

He nodded quickly and stepped back.

Across the camp, Lena adjusted one of the supports beneath an injured patient, her movements careful, deliberate. "We need more light," she said.

Fredrick glanced up. "We'll use what we have from the shuttle," he said. "Once it's fully stable."

William shook his head slightly. "Light will help," he said. "But it won't solve the problem."

Fredrick looked at him. "What will?"

William didn't answer right away.

He watched the fog.

Measured it.

Felt the pattern in it.

"Understanding it," he said finally.

Silas gave a low laugh from the edge of the group. "That's comforting."

Tarin didn't laugh. "He's not wrong," he said.

The last of the daylight slipped behind the ridge.

The canyon darkened from the ground up.

The fog thickened with it.

Within minutes, the lower half of the shuttle was no longer clearly visible, its outline blurred, its edges uncertain. The upper hull remained distinct against the narrow strip of sky, but even that began to soften as the light faded.

"Watch positions," Alex said. "Now."

Fredrick nodded. "I'll take first with—" he glanced around, then pointed. "You."

A man near the edge of the group stepped forward.

They moved to opposite sides of the camp, not far—no more than a few steps beyond the central area—but enough to give coverage.

"Stay within sight," Alex said.

Fredrick nodded. "We will."

William watched them take position.

Then stepped back toward the center.

The group settled.

Not comfortably.

But intentionally.

Voices lowered.

Movement reduced.

Attention sharpened.

Time shifted.

Minutes felt longer.

Sound changed.

Small noises—movement of cloth, a shift of stone, the quiet exhale of breath—seemed louder, closer, then suddenly farther away.

At one point, a voice from the edge of the camp called out, "I heard something."

Fredrick's voice came back, but from a direction that didn't quite match where he stood. "What did you hear?"

"I don't know," the man said. "Movement."

William listened.

Not to the words.

To the pattern.

Then he spoke.

"Nothing is approaching," he said.

The man hesitated. "How do you know?"

William looked out into the fog. "Because the sound is not moving toward us," he said. "It's reflecting."

There was a pause.

Then the man nodded, though it was unclear if he fully understood.

The fog rose higher.

Knee level.

Then waist.

The edges of the camp were no longer clear.

Only the center held.

Alex sat beside one of the injured, her posture steady despite the strain of the day. Lena worked quietly beside her, adjusting bandages, checking breathing, doing what she could with what they had.

Fredrick returned from his position after the first interval, his expression thoughtful. "You lose your sense of direction out there," he said quietly to William. "Even standing still."

"Yes."

Fredrick shook his head slightly. "I don't like that."

"No."

Silas moved closer to the center, no longer standing at the edge. He said nothing, but his earlier confidence had shifted into something more measured.

Tarin sat on a low stone, his eyes moving constantly, tracking what little could still be seen.

Darren remained standing.

Watching.

Always watching.

William stood near the center of the camp, his attention still on the pattern.

The fog.

The sound.

The way the environment reshaped perception itself.

This was not just an obstacle.

It was a condition.

A system.

And they were inside it.

Alex looked up at him. "We can't operate in this," she said quietly.

"No," he said.

Fredrick glanced between them. "Then what do we do?"

William's gaze lifted briefly to the narrow strip of sky above them.

Clear.

Unobstructed.

Then back down to the fog.

"We don't stay here," he said.

The words settled into the space between them.

Not immediate.

Not urgent.

But certain.

Alex held his gaze for a moment.

Then nodded once.

"Not yet," she said. "But soon."

William inclined his head slightly.

Around them, the camp held.

Barely visible beyond a few steps.

Defined more by presence than by sight.

Above them, the sky remained open.

Below—

The canyon filled.

And the night deepened around them.

## Chapter 10 - Morning Assessment

Morning did not arrive in the canyon the way it had at Outpost Meridian.

There was light.

But it came slowly.

Not from above.

From within.

The fog thinned first.

Not cleared—thinned.

What had been dense and close through the night loosened its hold, drawing upward in layers that revealed shapes in stages rather than all at once. The nearest ground returned first. Then the edges of the camp. Then the lower half of the shuttle, still tilted where it had come to rest.

The sky remained a narrow strip above them, pale and distant.

Alex was already awake.

She had not slept long—no one had—but she had rested enough to continue. She moved quietly through the camp, checking positions, reassessing injuries, adjusting supports where the night had shifted things out of alignment.

"How is it?" she asked Lena in a low voice.

Lena looked up from where she knelt beside one of the injured. "Stable," she said. "Not better. But not worse."

Alex nodded once. "That's what we need right now."

Nearby, Fredrick Mercer pushed himself upright from where he had been sitting—pausing halfway as if steadying himself—before finishing the motion and stepping toward the center of the camp. He took in the space with a practiced eye—the positions, the people, the small changes that had taken place overnight.

"Still with us," he said quietly.

"For now," Alex replied.

William stood a short distance away, already awake, already observing.

The fog had not left.

It had simply changed.

Where it had been dense and enclosing during the night, it now clung in uneven patches across the canyon floor, lingering longer in the lower ground, lifting more quickly along the slight rises. The pattern was consistent.

Predictable.

He watched it.

Measured it.

Then turned his attention to the group.

"Count," he said.

Fredrick nodded immediately. "Right."

They moved through the camp again, as they had the day before.

Name.

Response.

Condition.

This time, the answers came more quickly.

People were more aware now.

More grounded in what had happened.

When they finished, Fredrick looked up. "Twenty-four," he said.

Alex's gaze shifted briefly toward the place where Jonas had been laid.

Then back again.

"Yes," she said.

William nodded once.

"Condition groups," he said.

Alex was already thinking in the same terms. "Critical, stable, functional," she said.

Fredrick gave a faint, approving smile. "I'm starting to like that system."

They moved through the group again, this time assigning more clearly.

Critical:

Two still at risk.

Breathing shallow.

Energy low.

Stable:

Several more.

Injured, but holding.

Functional:

The rest.

Enough to work.

Enough to move.

That mattered.

Alex stood and looked across the camp. "We need to establish a full inventory," she said. "Water, food, tools, anything we can use."

Fredrick nodded. "Agreed."

William glanced toward the shuttle. "We can access it now," he said. "The pressure has dropped."

Darren Kroll, standing nearby, nodded slightly. "It's stable enough," he said. "Not safe forever. But safe enough."

Alex looked at him briefly, then at William. "We go in carefully," she said. "No one alone."

"Yes."

They assembled a small team.

William.

Alex.

Darren.

Fredrick.

Two others to carry.

Silas stepped forward, unasked. "You'll want muscle," he said.

Alex considered for a fraction of a second.

Then nodded. "Stay with the group. Follow instructions."

Silas gave a short grin. "Always do."

Tarin remained where he was, watching the edges of the canyon. "I'll keep an eye out here," he said. "Things look different this morning."

William glanced at him. "Yes," he said.

They moved toward the shuttle.

In daylight—what passed for it here—the damage was clearer.

The hull had held.

But barely.

Scrapes along the underside had exposed structural seams.

One of the side panels had shifted out of alignment.

The rear section—where the hiss had been—now stood quiet, the pressure fully released.

William paused at the hatch.

Listened.

Nothing.

Then stepped inside.

The interior felt colder.

Not physically.

Functionally.

Dead systems.

Silent panels.

No movement.

Alex moved past him, already focused. "Medical storage first," she said. "Then water, then tools."

Darren moved with her, efficient, precise.

Fredrick followed, scanning for anything they might have missed the day before.

Silas moved through the space with more force, pulling loose panels free, clearing access where needed.

"Careful," Alex said once, not sharply, but firmly.

Silas slowed slightly. "Got it."

They worked.

Not rushing.

But not wasting time.

Water containers.

Food packs.

Med kits.

Tools.

Each item carried out and passed down the line to those waiting outside.

William moved toward the forward section, checking the structure again.

The cockpit remained intact.

But dead.

No power.

No signal.

No immediate recovery.

He studied it for a moment longer.

Then turned away.

Outside, the group began organizing what was brought out.

Alex directed without hesitation. "Water here. Food separate. Medical stays with me."

Lena followed her lead, arranging supplies into clean, usable groups.

Fredrick stepped back once they were clear of the shuttle, looking over what they had gathered. "This will last," he said, "if we manage it."

"For how long?" someone asked.

Fredrick hesitated.

William answered.

"Long enough to make the next decision matter," he said.

The group fell quiet.

Alex looked at him. "Then we make that decision soon."

"Yes."

Fredrick folded his arms loosely. "Which is?"

William stepped forward, his gaze moving from the camp… to the canyon walls… to the fog still lingering in the lower ground.

"We don't stay here," he said.

This time, the words reached further.

The group heard them.

Felt them.

Gideon Trask stepped forward from where he had been standing. "And go where?" he asked.

William looked up.

Not at the walls.

Beyond them.

"To higher ground," he said.

Gideon followed his gaze. "That's a climb," he said.

"Yes."

"With injured," Gideon added.

"Yes."

Gideon considered that, then shook his head slightly. "We have shelter here," he said. "Supplies. The shuttle. We can stabilize, signal for rescue—"

"The signal will not hold here," William said.

Gideon's expression tightened slightly. "You don't know that."

William met his gaze. "Yes," he said. "I do."

There was no force in it.

No challenge.

Just certainty.

Gideon held that for a moment.

Then looked away.

Fredrick stepped in, not to argue, but to steady the moment. "Let's understand the situation fully before we commit," he said. "We've just gotten through the first night."

Alex nodded. "We assess. Then we decide."

William inclined his head slightly.

But his gaze returned once more to the canyon walls.

To the fog that still lingered.

To the pattern that had already begun to reveal itself.

This place—

This canyon—

Was not stable.

Not for what they needed.

Not for what was coming.

The group returned to their tasks.

Sorting.

Organizing.

Stabilizing.

But something had shifted.

Not in the environment.

In the understanding of it.

They were not simply stranded.

They were in the wrong place.

And staying—

Was no longer a neutral choice.

Above them, the strip of sky widened slightly as the fog continued to lift.

For a few hours, the canyon would feel almost manageable.

Almost open.

But William knew what came next.

It would return.

It always did.

And when it did—

They would need to be ready to move.

## Chapter 11 - First Signal

By midmorning, the canyon felt almost manageable.

The fog had lifted to a thin, uneven layer that clung to the lowest ground, leaving most of the camp visible again. The air was clearer. The sound more reliable. The sense of confinement had eased just enough to make movement possible without hesitation.

It was, William knew, the most deceptive part of the cycle.

Alex stood near the center of the camp, reviewing the supplies they had organized. "Water is better than I expected," she said. "Food is limited, but workable. Medical is… enough, if nothing else goes wrong."

Fredrick gave a quiet breath. "Let's hope nothing else goes wrong."

Alex didn't respond to that.

Instead, she looked toward the small cluster of salvaged equipment Darren had set aside earlier. "If we're going to test communication," she said, "this is the window."

William nodded. "Yes."

The group had begun to settle into a rhythm—small tasks, quiet movement, focused effort. The shock of the crash had passed. The reality of their situation had not.

Gideon Trask stepped forward as Alex and William approached the equipment. "You think you can reach Meridian from here?" he asked.

William glanced at the canyon walls, then back to the device. "Not consistently," he said. "But we may be able to send a partial signal."

Gideon folded his arms. "Partial isn't much."

"It's more than none," Alex said.

Fredrick joined them, his expression sharpening with interest. "What do you need?" he asked.

William knelt beside the equipment, opening the casing with practiced ease. "Power first," he said. "Then alignment."

Darren was already there, crouched on the opposite side. He didn't wait to be asked.

"This unit wasn't designed for this environment," he said, running his fingers lightly along the internal connections. "We'll get interference from multiple directions."

"Yes," William said. "We compensate for timing, not strength."

Darren glanced at him, then nodded once. "That makes sense."

Alex looked between them. "Tell me what to adjust."

William pointed to a narrow relay strip inside the unit. "This needs to shift," he said. "Not much. Just enough to anticipate the delay."

Alex reached in carefully, adjusting the component with steady precision. "Here?"

"A little more."

She made the change.

Darren moved to the secondary connection. "If we don't stabilize this," he said, "the signal will fragment."

William nodded. "Do it."

Fredrick watched them, a faint, almost incredulous expression crossing his face. "You two work like you've been doing this together for years," he said.

Alex didn't look up. "Feels like it," she said.

The group gathered at a distance—not crowding, but watching.

Hope was a quiet thing here.

No one said much.

No one wanted to risk it.

William made a final adjustment, then sat back slightly. "We try now," he said.

Alex looked at Fredrick. "You should make the call."

Fredrick blinked. "Me?"

"Yes."

He hesitated.

Then nodded.

"Right," he said quietly.

He leaned toward the unit, taking the receiver in hand. For a moment, he said nothing, as if gathering the right words.

Then—

"Outpost Meridian, this is Fredrick Mercer," he said. "Emergency transmission. Respond if you can."

The signal went out.

For a second—

Nothing.

Then—

A faint return.

Static.

Not clean.

Not stable.

But there.

Fredrick's head lifted slightly. "We've got something," he said.

The static shifted.

A fragment of sound.

Then—

"…—idian…rece—…repeat—"

It cut out.

Alex leaned forward. "Again."

Fredrick nodded. "Outpost Meridian, this is Mercer. Emergency transmission from shuttle down. Do you copy?"

The unit flickered.

The signal strained.

Then—

"…Merc—…read—…partial…location—"

It broke apart.

Silence.

Fredrick exhaled slowly. "They heard something," he said.

William nodded. "Yes."

Gideon stepped closer. "That's not enough," he said.

"No," William agreed. "But it confirms connection."

Alex sat back slightly. "We can refine it," she said. "Stabilize the timing."

Darren shook his head once. "Not here," he said.

Alex looked at him. "Why?"

Darren gestured toward the canyon. "Too much interference," he said. "It's not just blocking the signal—it's distorting it."

William nodded. "Yes."

Fredrick looked between them. "You're saying this is as good as it gets?"

"Here," William said.

The word settled.

Gideon's expression tightened. "Then we need more power," he said. "Boost the signal. Force it through."

"That won't work," Alex said.

"Why not?"

"Because it's not a strength problem," she replied. "It's a timing problem."

Gideon shook his head. "A stronger signal cuts through interference."

"Not this kind," William said.

Gideon turned to him. "Then what kind is it?"

William met his gaze. "Environmental," he said. "Layered. Variable. The signal doesn't just weaken—it shifts."

Gideon frowned. "Meaning?"

"It arrives out of sync," William said. "Fragments. Delayed. Overlapping."

Fredrick gave a quiet breath. "That's exactly what we saw on the network."

"Yes," William said.

Alex looked toward the canyon walls again. "And it's worse here."

"Yes."

The group fell silent.

The answer was becoming clearer.

Not all at once.

But enough.

Tarin stepped closer, his expression thoughtful. "So if the problem is the environment," he said, "then the solution isn't the device."

"No," William said.

Tarin nodded slowly. "It's the location."

"Yes."

Gideon looked up toward the ridge line. "Higher ground," he said.

William inclined his head slightly.

Fredrick ran a hand across his face. "That's a long way up," he said.

"Yes."

"With injured," Fredrick added.

"Yes."

Alex stood. "Then we plan it properly," she said.

Gideon looked at her. "Or we stay and try again."

Alex met his gaze. "And lose the signal again tonight?"

Gideon didn't answer.

Because he knew.

They all did.

The fog would return.

The pattern would repeat.

And this—

This brief window—

Would close.

Darren adjusted the unit slightly, then powered it down. "We can make it work better," he said. "Just not here."

William nodded. "We prepare to move."

Fredrick looked at the group, then back at William. "Soon," he said.

"Yes."

The word carried more weight now.

Not just a decision.

A direction.

Around them, the canyon remained quiet.

The fog lingered in the lowest ground, waiting.

Above, the sky stretched clear.

Unobstructed.

Reachable.

For now.

Alex looked at William. "We'll need a route," she said.

William's gaze lifted toward the ridge.

Then beyond it.

"Yes," he said.

"We will."

## Chapter 12 - Signal Failure

By midday, the canyon felt almost open.

The fog had thinned to scattered patches along the lowest ground, barely noticeable unless you were looking for it. The air was clearer. Sound traveled more normally. Movement no longer required careful calculation with every step.

It would have been easy to believe the worst had passed.

Some of the group did.

A few had moved slightly farther from the central camp, testing the boundaries they had marked the day before. Others spoke a little more freely, voices rising just enough to suggest that the immediate danger had eased.

William watched that.

Not with concern.

With recognition.

"This is the window," Alex said, stepping up beside him.

"Yes."

She crossed her arms lightly. "We need to use it."

"We will."

She glanced toward the equipment they had used earlier. "One more attempt," she said.

William nodded. "Yes."

They moved back toward the signal unit.

Darren was already there.

He had not strayed far from it since the first attempt, his attention returning to it repeatedly, not out of restlessness, but out of focus.

"I've adjusted the timing offset," he said as they approached. "It should hold longer."

Alex crouched beside him. "How much longer?"

Darren gave a slight shrug. "Enough to try."

William knelt opposite him. "We begin now."

Fredrick joined them again, slower this time, but no less steady. "Let's see if we can do better than partial," he said.

Gideon stood nearby, arms folded, watching.

The rest of the group gathered at a distance, as before.

Not close.

Not crowding.

But present.

Hope had not grown louder.

It had grown quieter.

More careful.

Alex powered the unit.

The display flickered once—

Then steadied.

Better than before.

"Signal is cleaner," she said.

"Yes," William replied.

Darren adjusted one final connection. "That's as good as it gets down here," he said.

Fredrick took the receiver again.

He didn't hesitate this time.

"Outpost Meridian, this is Mercer," he said. "Emergency transmission from downed shuttle. Do you copy?"

The signal went out.

The unit held.

For a second—

Two—

Then—

"…Mercer…reading…partial…"

The voice was clearer.

Not clean.

But clearer.

Fredrick leaned forward slightly. "Meridian, we are alive," he said. "Twenty-four survivors. Multiple injuries. Location uncertain. Do you copy?"

The response came back, fragmented but stronger.

"…copy…repeat…twenty-four…confirm…location…"

Alex looked at William. "They're getting more of it."

"Yes."

Darren watched the signal line. "It's holding," he said.

For a moment—

It did.

The line steadied.

The sound aligned.

Hope lifted.

Just enough.

Fredrick spoke again. "Meridian, we are in a canyon region. Low elevation. Signal unstable. We will attempt to transmit coordinates—"

The unit flickered.

Once.

Twice.

The line shifted.

William's gaze sharpened. "It's slipping."

Darren leaned in. "No—hold on—"

The signal fractured.

"…—anyon…repeat…coor—"

Static surged.

The line collapsed.

The display broke into overlapping fragments—

Then went dark.

Silence.

Fredrick held the receiver a moment longer.

As if waiting.

Then lowered it slowly.

Alex stared at the unit. "No," she said quietly. "We had it."

Darren shook his head. "Not long enough."

Gideon stepped forward. "Try again."

Alex looked up. "It won't hold."

"Try anyway."

William shook his head. "No."

Gideon turned to him. "We were close."

"Yes."

"Then we push it."

"That will make it worse," William said.

Gideon's expression tightened. "You don't know that."

"Yes," William said. "I do."

There was no force in it.

No challenge.

Just certainty.

Gideon held his gaze.

Then looked back at the unit.

Frustration surfaced—not loud, not uncontrolled—but present.

"We were right there," he said.

Alex sat back slightly. "We confirmed contact," she said. "That matters."

"It's not enough," Gideon replied.

"No," she said. "It's not."

The group behind them had gone quiet again.

Hope had risen—

And fallen.

Faster this time.

Fredrick exhaled slowly, the breath lingering a fraction longer than it should have.

"They know we're alive," he said.

He paused, just briefly.

"Just… tired."

"Yes," William replied.

"They'll start searching."

"Yes."

Fredrick nodded once. "That gives us time."

"It gives us a window," Alex said.

William looked toward the canyon walls.

The light had begun to shift.

Subtly.

But enough.

The fog was returning.

Not yet visible.

But present.

The pattern was repeating.

"It's already closing," he said.

Alex followed his gaze.

She saw it now.

Not the fog itself—

The change before it.

The air.

The way the lower ground lost clarity first.

"How long?" she asked.

"Hours," William said. "Less here than above."

Gideon turned. "Above," he said.

William nodded.

Fredrick looked between them. "You're both thinking the same thing."

"Yes," Alex said.

Gideon folded his arms again, but there was less resistance in the gesture now. "We can try again tomorrow," he said.

William shook his head.

"No," he said.

Gideon frowned. "Why not?"

William met his gaze. "Because tomorrow will be the same," he said. "And the next day."

Alex added quietly, "And the signal will fail the same way."

Gideon looked at the canyon walls.

Then up.

Toward the ridge.

Higher ground.

He didn't argue.

Not this time.

Fredrick nodded slowly. "Then we don't wait," he said.

"No," William said.

"We move."

The word settled across the group.

Not sudden.

Not forced.

But real.

The direction had been forming.

Now it had taken shape.

Alex stood. "We prepare this afternoon," she said. "We don't move in fog. We move in the window."

William nodded. "Yes."

Darren looked at the unit one last time, then powered it down completely. "It'll work better up there," he said.

William glanced at him. "Yes."

Darren gave a slight nod.

Not pride.

Not satisfaction.

Just understanding.

Tarin stepped closer, his expression thoughtful. "You'll need a path," he said.

William looked at him. "Yes."

Tarin nodded toward the canyon wall. "There's always one," he said. "It's just not always obvious."

Silas gave a short breath. "Or easy."

"No," Tarin said. "Not easy."

Fredrick looked at the group.

Then at the rising shadow along the canyon floor.

"We don't have much time," he said.

"No," Alex replied.

William's gaze lifted once more toward the ridge above.

The sky beyond it.

Clear.

Reachable.

For now.

"Then we begin," he said.

And this time—

No one disagreed.

## Chapter 13 - Fredrick's Passing

The light did not hold as long as it had the day before.

By early afternoon, the edges of the canyon had already begun to soften again, the lower ground losing definition in that same quiet, deliberate way. The fog was returning—earlier, thicker, more certain.

Alex noticed it first.

Then William.

Fredrick saw it a moment later.

"Well," he said softly, looking toward the base of the canyon wall, "it's not waiting for us to be ready."

"No," William said. "It won't."

The camp had shifted into preparation.

Not movement yet.

But direction.

Supplies had been sorted into carry groups. Water redistributed. Food divided. The injured reassessed—again—not just for stability, but for transport.

Alex moved between them with steady focus. "We need to know who can be moved," she said. "And how."

Lena followed her, recording what she could.

"This one can be supported," Alex said quietly. "Two people. No sudden movement."

"And Jonas—" Lena stopped herself.

Alex's expression didn't change. "Jonas stays," she said. "We mark the location."

Lena nodded.

It was not cold.

It was necessary.

Fredrick stood a short distance away, watching the preparations take shape. There was a quiet pride in his expression—not in the situation, but in how the group had responded to it.

They were organizing.

Adapting.

Becoming something more than passengers.

He took a step forward—

Then stopped.

Just slightly.

His hand moved, almost unconsciously, to his side.

William saw it.

A small thing.

But not random.

"Fredrick," he said.

Fredrick looked up. "I'm fine," he said, almost automatically.

William didn't respond.

He stepped closer.

Fredrick straightened, as if correcting posture alone would resolve whatever had shifted. "Just a bit stiff from the landing," he added. "Nothing to—"

He stopped.

Not dramatically.

Not sharply.

But enough.

Alex was already moving.

"Sit," she said.

Fredrick gave a faint smile. "You're starting to sound like me."

"Sit," she repeated.

This time, he did.

Slowly.

Carefully.

Alex knelt beside him, her hands already working—checking pulse, breathing, response.

"What is it?" Fredrick asked, quieter now.

Alex didn't answer right away.

William stood just behind her, watching.

Not guessing.

Observing.

"Internal," Alex said finally.

Fredrick exhaled slowly. "I was hoping you wouldn't say that."

Alex met his gaze. "When did it start?"

He considered that.

"After the second impact," he said. "I thought it was just… strain."

He gave a faint breath.

"Should've known better."

Alex nodded slightly. "It wasn't."

Fredrick gave a small, almost amused breath. "That figures."

Around them, the movement of the camp slowed.

Not stopped.

But slowed.

People noticed.

They always did.

Alex adjusted her position, her voice steady but quieter now. "You need to stay still," she said. "No movement."

Fredrick looked past her, toward the group. "That's not very helpful timing," he said.

"No," Alex replied. "It isn't."

William stepped forward slightly. "You need to conserve energy," he said.

Fredrick glanced at him. "You're telling me to sit out the most important part?"

"Yes."

Fredrick held his gaze.

Then gave a small nod.

"All right," he said. "I suppose I've earned at least one bad day."

Alex's expression softened—just slightly.

She adjusted his position, supporting him more fully, reducing strain.

"Better?" she asked.

"Yes," Fredrick said.

He wasn't lying.

But he wasn't telling the full truth either.

William saw that.

And understood it.

The fog continued to build.

Higher now.

Closer.

The boundary stones began to fade again.

Time was shortening.

Alex remained beside Fredrick, her hands still, her attention focused. There was nothing more she could do to change the outcome.

Only manage it.

Fredrick seemed to understand that.

He looked at her. "You've done well," he said.

Alex shook her head slightly. "Not finished yet."

Fredrick smiled faintly. "No," he said. "You're not."

He turned his head slightly toward William.

"You saw it first," he said.

William didn't answer immediately.

Then, simply: "Yes."

Fredrick nodded. "You always do."

There was no accusation in it.

No regret.

Just recognition.

Fredrick shifted his gaze toward the group—the people moving, organizing, preparing.

"They'll follow you," he said quietly.

William looked at him.

"They already are," Fredrick added.

Alex glanced between them, but said nothing.

Fredrick's breathing changed.

Not suddenly.

Gradually.

Each breath slightly shallower than the last—

as if something inside him had begun to let go.

Alex adjusted her position again, her voice calm. "Stay with me," she said.

"I am," Fredrick replied.

He looked at William again.

"Don't wait too long," he said.

His voice was quieter now. Not weaker—just… farther away.

William inclined his head slightly.

"I won't."

Fredrick's expression eased.

Satisfied.

He looked once more toward the canyon walls, where the fog now moved more visibly, rising, thickening, closing.

"Strange place," he said softly.

"Yes," William replied.

Fredrick gave a faint breath that might have been a laugh.

Then—

Stillness.

Not abrupt.

Not violent.

Just—

Complete.

Alex remained where she was for a moment longer.

Then she exhaled slowly and lowered her head.

"I'm sorry," she said quietly.

No one spoke.

The canyon held the moment.

Again.

But this time—

It felt heavier.

Fredrick had not just been part of the group.

He had been part of its structure.

Its center.

And now—

That had shifted.

Alex rose slowly.

Her expression was composed.

But changed.

She looked at William.

"It's you now," she said.

It wasn't a question.

William nodded once.

"Yes."

He stepped forward.

Not dramatically.

Not forcefully.

But clearly.

"Everyone," he said.

The group turned.

Movement slowed.

Attention focused.

"We continue," he said.

The same words as before.

But now—

They carried more weight.

"We prepare to move," he continued. "We do not wait for conditions to improve. They will not."

No one argued.

Not Gideon.

Not Silas.

Not anyone.

The direction was clear.

Because the cost of waiting had just been made real.

Alex moved back into position beside the injured.

Lena followed.

The group resumed motion.

But it was different now.

More focused.

More deliberate.

Less uncertain.

Above them, the strip of sky narrowed as the fog rose.

Around them, the canyon began to close again.

And at the center of it—

The group moved forward.

Without Fredrick.

But not without direction.

## Chapter 14 - The Argument

The fog rose faster that afternoon.

Not dramatically.

But enough that no one could ignore it.

The lower ground blurred first, the boundary stones fading into soft shapes that were harder to track with each passing minute. The canyon walls lost definition near their base, as if the world itself had decided to remove detail from the places that mattered most.

The group felt it.

Not just in sight.

In pressure.

In time.

Alex stood near the center of the camp, finishing a final check on the injured. Her movements were efficient, controlled—but there was a sharper edge now. Not urgency. Direction.

"We move in the next window," she said, standing. "We organize now."

Several heads nodded.

Not all.

Gideon Trask stepped forward.

"We need to talk about that," he said.

The words weren't loud.

But they carried.

William turned slightly toward him.

"So let's talk," Gideon continued. "Because what you're proposing—moving this entire group, including the injured, up that wall—" he gestured toward the canyon ridge "—is not a small decision."

"No," William said.

"It's a dangerous one."

"Yes."

Gideon paused.

That wasn't the resistance he expected.

"It's more dangerous than staying," he said.

William shook his head.

"No," he said.

Gideon's jaw tightened slightly. "You don't know that."

"Yes," William said. "I do."

There it was again.

Not force.

Not challenge.

Certainty.

Gideon took a step closer. "Then explain it," he said.

A few others shifted.

Not away.

Toward.

This mattered.

William didn't raise his voice.

He didn't change his tone.

"The environment here is unstable," he said. "The fog reduces visibility, distorts sound, and interferes with signal. It returns earlier each cycle. It builds from the lowest ground upward."

Gideon crossed his arms. "We can adapt to that."

"For a time," William said.

"That's all we need," Gideon replied. "Time. They know we're alive. They'll come looking."

William nodded once.

"Yes," he said.

"Then we wait," Gideon said.

William looked at him.

"Rescue will not reach us here," he said.

Gideon's expression hardened. "You don't know that."

William's gaze didn't shift.

"The canyon restricts access," he said. "Landing is limited. Visibility is inconsistent. Signal is unreliable. Search patterns will prioritize open terrain."

Gideon shook his head. "You're assuming—"

"I'm observing," William said.

That stopped him.

Just for a moment.

Alex stepped in—not to interrupt, but to anchor. "We tested the signal," she said. "It failed. Not because of the device. Because of the location."

Gideon glanced at her. "And it almost worked."

"It held for seconds," Alex said. "Not long enough to send coordinates. Not long enough to guide rescue."

Gideon turned back to William. "Then we try again."

William shook his head.

"No," he said.

"Why?"

"Because the pattern will repeat," William said. "And each cycle reduces our margin."

Gideon exhaled sharply. "Margin for what?"

William's gaze shifted briefly toward the fog, now rising higher along the canyon floor.

"For error," he said.

Silence settled.

Not agreement.

But recognition.

Gideon wasn't finished.

"You're asking injured people to climb," he said. "You're asking everyone to carry supplies, move through unstable terrain, and trust that there's a path we can actually use."

"Yes," William said.

Gideon let out a short breath. "That's a lot of risk."

"Yes."

"And if you're wrong?"

William met his gaze.

"Then we fail faster," he said.

The words landed.

Harder than anything else he had said.

Gideon stared at him.

"You're willing to risk that?" he asked.

William didn't hesitate.

"Yes."

Gideon shook his head. "That's not leadership," he said. "That's—"

He stopped.

Searching for the word.

Alex said it for him.

"Reality," she said.

Gideon looked at her.

She didn't look away.

"We've already seen what staying does," she continued. "We lose time. We lose signal. We lose people."

Gideon's eyes flicked briefly—just briefly—toward where Fredrick had been.

Then back.

"That doesn't mean we rush into something worse," he said.

"No," Alex agreed. "It means we choose the better risk."

Gideon let that sit.

Across the group, others were listening now.

Not passively.

Measuring.

Deciding.

Tarin stepped forward slightly. "There's always a way out of terrain like this," he said. "It's just not always obvious."

Gideon looked at him. "And you know where it is?"

Tarin shook his head. "Not yet."

"That's not reassuring."

"It's honest," Tarin replied.

Silas gave a quiet snort. "Honest doesn't get us up that wall."

"No," Tarin said. "But it gets us looking in the right place."

Darren spoke then.

Quietly.

From where he stood near the edge of the group.

"The signal will never work here," he said.

All eyes turned to him.

Gideon frowned. "You don't know that."

Darren met his gaze.

"I do," he said.

There was no force in it.

No challenge.

Just… agreement.

With William.

Gideon looked between them.

Then at the canyon.

Then up.

Toward the ridge.

The space above.

Open.

Clear.

Reachable.

The fog continued to rise.

Now at knee height.

Then higher.

Closing the lower ground again.

William stepped forward.

Not aggressively.

Not dramatically.

Just—

Clearly.

"We move because staying removes options," he said. "Movement creates them."

He let that sit.

Then added:

"We move in stages. We carry what we can. We support the injured. We establish positions along the route."

Gideon listened.

Not agreeing yet.

But no longer resisting.

Alex stepped beside William. "We plan it," she said. "We don't rush it. But we don't delay it either."

Fredrick's absence was felt in that moment.

Where he would have spoken—

They now held the space.

Gideon exhaled slowly.

Then nodded once.

Not fully convinced.

But committed enough.

"All right," he said. "We plan it."

The shift was subtle.

But complete.

The fog rose higher.

The window narrowed.

The decision had been made.

Now—

They had to make it work.

Night would come soon.

And the canyon had not finished with them yet.

## Chapter 15 - The Night Pressure

Night came earlier than any of them wanted.

The fog began gathering before the last of the light had fully slipped from the narrow strip of sky above, rising first along the edges of the canyon floor and then spreading inward in that same quiet, relentless way they had already begun to dread. It did not rush. It did not sweep in. It simply built—layer on layer—until the lower stones of the boundary line softened and the far edge of the shuttle blurred into a shape rather than an object.

The camp tightened in response.

Not by order.

By instinct.

People moved closer to the center without being told, their voices lowering as if the fog itself demanded less sound. The injured had been settled as securely as Alex and Lena could manage. The supplies most critical for the morning had been grouped near the middle of camp where they could be reached quickly. What little could be done tonight had been done.

Now there was only waiting.

And listening.

Alex sat near the medical cluster, one knee drawn up slightly, her posture steady despite the long day. She had checked each injured person twice in the last hour, made what adjustments she could, and now watched the camp with the look of someone who understood that rest was necessary but sleep would not come easily.

William stood a short distance beyond the center, close enough to hear the group, far enough to watch the boundary.

He had not moved much in the last several minutes.

That, more than anything, made some of the others uneasy.

When William became still, it usually meant he was listening to something other people had not yet noticed.

Tarin Jex sat on a low stone near the edge of the camp, his elbows resting lightly on his knees, his eyes moving from one patch of fog to another. Silas Venn remained standing, though no longer at the outer line. The confidence he had shown earlier had narrowed into caution. Darren Kroll stood near the signal equipment they had powered down before dusk, his attention turning outward now that the machine could do nothing more for them until morning.

Gideon Trask sat with his back against a salvaged panel, one forearm across his knee, his expression unreadable in the dim light.

No one spoke for a while.

The camp held itself together in the darkening canyon, each person measuring the same thing in a different way.

The fog climbed higher.

Ankle height.

Then knee.

By the time the last clean edge of daylight had vanished, the world beyond the center of camp no longer felt like distance.

It felt like uncertainty given shape.

A quiet scraping sound came from somewhere beyond the marked stones.

Not loud.

Just enough to matter.

Several heads turned at once.

Silas straightened. “You hear that?”

No one answered immediately.

The sound came again.

A shift of stone.

A light, uneven drag.

Then stillness.

Alex rose slowly to her feet. "No one leaves the boundary," she said.

Her voice was calm.

But the camp changed around it.

Not panicked.

Alert.

William did not turn.

His eyes remained on the fog beyond the nearest stones.

Then—

The first growl.

Low.

Distant enough that no one could say for certain where it had come from.

It did not echo the way a human voice did. It seemed to move through the fog rather than bounce off it, arriving in the camp as a vibration more than a sound.

One of the younger technicians swore under his breath.

Another drew in a quick breath and held it.

Gideon pushed himself upright without speaking.

Silas looked out into the fog and tried for a smile that did not quite settle. "Well," he said quietly, "that sounds promising."

Tarin did not take his eyes off the boundary. "No," he said. "It doesn't."

The sound came again.

Closer this time.

Or perhaps just clearer.

That was the problem.

No one could tell.

Alex moved one step nearer the center of the camp. "Stay together," she said. "No one drifts."

Fredrick's absence was felt sharply in moments like that. The camp had become used to his steadying voice moving among them, making tension smaller simply by giving it order. Without him, the silence between one sound and the next seemed wider.

William finally spoke.

"Listen to the interval," he said.

Gideon turned slightly. "The interval?"

"Yes."

Another sound came from the fog.

Not a growl this time.

A short, sharp huff of breath.

Then the soft shift of something moving over rock.

Not heavy enough to be a herd animal.

Not light enough to ignore.

William's gaze tracked the sound.

"It's circling," he said.

Silas looked at him. "One?"

William did not answer right away.

Then—

A second growl.

From a different direction.

Closer to the opposite side of camp.

Not loud.

But unmistakable.

The group tightened again.

This time visibly.

Lena moved closer to the injured without thinking about it. One of the guards shifted position, no longer watching the prisoners at all. Tarin rose from his stone. Darren did not move, but his eyes sharpened.

Gideon's expression changed.

Not dramatically.

But enough.

This was no longer theory.

No longer William's projection of risk onto terrain and weather.

Something was out there.

Watching.

Testing.

Alex's voice stayed level. "How many?"

William watched the fog.

"More than one," he said.

The fog thickened another degree, as if encouraged by the dark.

The line of stones at the edge of camp had nearly disappeared now except where the nearest light caught them. Beyond that, the canyon had become shape without depth, presence without detail.

A stone shifted just outside the line.

Everyone heard it.

No one moved.

Then, in the dim light, something passed through the fog.

Not fully visible.

Not enough to name.

Just a darker motion within the gray.

Low to the ground.

Fast.

Gone.

One of the injured men let out a frightened breath.

Alex turned her head slightly. "Stay still," she said. "Stay quiet."

The camp obeyed.

Another moment passed.

Then another.

The fog moved softly in front of them, giving nothing back.

Silas leaned forward a fraction. "I don't like not seeing what's making that sound."

"That's the advantage," Tarin said.

"For them," Gideon added.

William gave the faintest nod.

"Yes."

The third sound did not come as a growl.

It came as a barked, snapping call from somewhere just beyond the edge of sight.

It was answered almost immediately from farther out in the canyon.

Not close enough to attack.

Close enough to coordinate.

The effect on the group was immediate.

Even those who had held themselves together well through the crash and the first night shifted under that sound. It wasn't only fear. It was recognition.

They were not alone down here.

And whatever moved in the canyon moved confidently.

Alex looked at William. "They know where we are."

"Yes."

Gideon stared into the fog. "They've probably known for a while."

No one argued with that.

Another movement.

This one slower.

More deliberate.

At the far edge of camp, where the boundary stones had nearly disappeared, the fog seemed to part around a shape that remained mostly hidden.

Then two points of reflected light appeared.

Low.

Still.

Watching.

No one spoke.

The eyes did not blink.

They held there for a long second—long enough for everyone in camp to see them, to know they were real, to understand that whatever stood just beyond sight had come close enough to judge the distance between itself and the people huddled in the center.

Then the shape shifted.

The eyes vanished.

The fog closed.

A few people exhaled all at once, as if only then remembering they had been holding their breath.

Gideon did not sit back down.

He remained standing, his gaze fixed on the place where the eyes had been.

The next sound came farther away.

Then another.

Then silence.

Not true silence.

The canyon never fully offered that.

But a retreating one.

A loosening.

As if the pressure had drawn back without leaving.

Tarin spoke first. "Testing us."

William nodded once.

"Yes."

Silas folded his arms again, but there was no humor left in the motion. "Then I'd say they got a decent look."

Alex remained where she was, still watching the boundary. "Will they come in?"

William considered the darkness for a moment.

"Not tonight," he said.

Gideon turned toward him. "How do you know?"

"They were close enough," William said. "If they intended to rush the camp, they would have done it before we were fully awake to them."

Tarin nodded slowly. "He's right."

That did not comfort anyone as much as it should have.

Because if the animals had chosen not to come in tonight, it meant choice was part of the pattern.

And choice meant intelligence.

Not human.

Not reasoning in any way that could be negotiated with.

But enough instinct and patience to make the canyon feel smaller than it already had.

The camp remained awake for a long time after that.

No one had to be told to stay within the center.

No one questioned the movement plan.

No one suggested trying the signal again tomorrow from the canyon floor.

The argument had ended.

Not with words.

With proof.

Late in the night, when the sounds had fully retreated and the fog had thickened so completely that the outer stones no longer existed except in memory, Gideon stepped closer to William.

His voice was low.

Quiet enough that most of the camp would not hear it.

"You were right," he said.

William did not look away from the fog. "Yes."

Under other circumstances, the answer might have sounded hard.

Here, it sounded like fact.

Gideon let out a slow breath. "I don't like that."

"No," William said. "You don't."

For a moment, that almost sounded like the beginning of a smile from someone else's life.

Then Gideon looked toward the dark edge of the camp again.

"We move at first light," he said.

William nodded once.

"Yes."

Gideon stood there a moment longer, then turned back toward the others.

And after that—

No one argued.

The canyon had made its case.

## Chapter 16 - Morning Evidence

Morning did not bring relief.

It brought clarity.

The fog had lifted again, rising slowly from the canyon floor and pulling back toward the base of the walls, leaving behind a space that looked almost unchanged from the day before.

Almost.

The camp stirred quietly.

No one spoke much at first. Movements were deliberate. Measured. The memory of the night still sat close—closer than sleep had pushed it away.

Alex was already awake, moving through the injured with quiet efficiency, checking each one, adjusting where needed. Lena followed, more confident now, anticipating what would be required before it was said.

William stood at the edge of the camp.

Watching.

Not the group.

The ground.

Tarin approached first.

He didn't speak right away.

He simply followed William's line of sight.

Then he saw it.

"Those weren't there yesterday," he said.

"No," William replied.

The marks began just beyond where the boundary stones had been set.

Subtle at first.

A disturbance in the loose rock.

A shift in the surface.

Then—

Clearer.

A series of impressions pressed into the softer patches between stone.

Not deep.

But deliberate.

Tarin crouched, studying them. "Not random," he said.

"No."

Tarin traced the edge of one with his eyes, not touching it. "Weight distributed," he added. "Not a single point. It's… controlled."

William nodded once.

Darren stepped closer, drawn without being called. He looked down, his expression tightening slightly—not in fear, but in recognition.

"They came right up to the line," he said.

"Yes."

Silas joined them, folding his arms as he looked down at the ground. "And decided not to come in," he said.

"For now," Tarin replied.

A few more people gathered.

Carefully.

No one stepped into the marked area.

Even though the stones were visible again, their meaning had changed.

Gideon arrived last.

He didn't ask what they were looking at.

He saw.

And that was enough.

He stood there for a moment, silent, his gaze moving from one mark to another, then outward—toward the canyon walls, toward the space that had hidden whatever had come that close during the night.

"They were here," he said.

"Yes," William replied.

Gideon nodded once.

No argument.

No hesitation.

Just acceptance.

Alex stepped up beside them. "How close?" she asked.

Tarin gestured lightly. "Closer than I like," he said.

Alex followed the line of the marks, then looked back toward the center of camp—toward the injured, toward the supplies, toward the people who would not be able to move quickly if something changed.

"That settles it," she said.

"Yes," William replied.

Fredrick's absence was felt again.

This would have been a moment he spoke into—turned into structure, into reassurance.

Now—

The evidence spoke for itself.

Gideon exhaled slowly. "We don't stay here," he said.

"No," William said.

Gideon looked up toward the ridge.

Then back at the marks.

Then at the group.

"We move," he said.

This time, it wasn't agreement.

It was decision.

The group began to shift almost immediately.

Not in panic.

In readiness.

Alex turned. "We prepare now," she said. "We move in the next window. No delays."

Lena nodded and moved.

Silas straightened, his earlier edge replaced by something more focused. "What's the plan?" he asked.

William looked toward the canyon wall.

Not randomly.

Specifically.

"The route is there," he said.

Tarin followed his gaze.

At first, it looked like nothing.

Just broken rock.

Uneven lines.

Then—

It became something else.

A pattern.

A series of angled rises.

Not straight.

Not obvious.

But possible.

Tarin gave a slow nod. "I see it," he said.

Darren looked next.

Then Gideon.

Silas squinted slightly. "That's not a path," he said.

"No," William replied.

"It's a way."

There was a difference.

And everyone felt it.

Alex stepped closer. "How long?" she asked.

William considered.

"Multiple stages," he said. "We establish positions as we go."

"With injured," she added.

"Yes."

Gideon folded his arms, but this time it wasn't resistance.

It was calculation.

"We'll need rotation," he said. "Carriers. Support. No one burns out early."

William nodded once.

"Agreed."

That was new.

Silas glanced between them. "Well," he said, "that's a pleasant change."

No one responded.

They didn't need to.

The structure was forming.

Not imposed.

Shared.

Darren stepped back slightly, his eyes moving from the route to the group. "We'll need to move weight in stages," he said. "Not everything at once."

William glanced at him.

"Yes," he said.

Darren gave a small nod.

Not proud.

Not hesitant.

Just… part of it now.

Alex turned toward the medical group. "We prioritize movement order," she said. "Critical cases first staging point, then rotation."

Lena followed immediately.

Tarin moved toward the base of the route, already studying footing, angles, where the rock held and where it didn't.

Silas picked up one of the larger support panels without being asked.

Gideon began organizing people into groups.

The camp changed.

Not slowly.

Clearly.

The marks in the ground remained visible behind them.

Not dramatic.

Not deep.

But undeniable.

William looked at them once more.

Then turned away.

"Torlan."

The name came quietly.

From Alex.

Not as a question.

As recognition.

He didn't respond right away.

Then—

A slight nod.

No explanation.

None needed.

He stepped forward.

Toward the base of the climb.

The others followed.

Behind them, the canyon remained.

The fog would return.

The marks would fade.

But the truth of them would not.

Ahead—

The wall waited.

And for the first time since the crash—

They were no longer reacting.

They were moving.

## Chapter 17 - Route Scouting

They did not begin the climb immediately.

That was the difference.

Before, they had reacted.

Now—

They prepared.

Torlan Tarsen stood at the base of the canyon wall, studying it in silence. What had looked like broken rock from below had begun to resolve into something else—a pattern of angled rises, shallow shelves, and narrow seams where the stone had fractured in ways that could be used.

Not a path.

A sequence.

Tarin stood a few steps to his left, scanning the same section. "It's there," he said quietly. "Just not where anyone would expect it."

Torlan nodded once.

Darren moved closer, his gaze shifting between sections. "That line won't hold weight," he said, indicating a sloped face of loose shale. "It'll give."

"Yes," Torlan said.

He pointed slightly higher. "There."

Tarin followed the gesture.

A narrow ledge—barely more than a foot wide—cut across the wall at an angle, disappearing behind a jut of stone before reappearing several meters farther along.

"That's not obvious," Tarin said.

"No."

"That's why it works."

Torlan stepped forward, placing his foot carefully against the base of the rock, testing it.

Solid.

He shifted weight.

Then withdrew.

"Not yet," Alex said behind him.

He glanced back.

She stood with her arms lightly folded, watching—not questioning.

"Just looking," he said.

"I know," she replied. "But if you go up there, you're going to keep going."

There was the faintest trace of something in her tone.

Not concern.

Understanding.

Torlan inclined his head slightly.

"Yes," he said.

She stepped closer, lowering her voice. "We need the whole route," she said. "Not just the first section."

"Yes."

Tarin nodded. "We scout it," he said. "All the way we can see—and as far as we can safely go."

Darren added, "And we find the failure points."

Torlan looked at him.

"Yes," he said.

Gideon approached, stopping just behind them. "You're taking a team?" he asked.

"Yes," Torlan replied.

Gideon nodded once. "Take who you need."

Silas stepped forward immediately. "I'm in," he said.

Tarin glanced at him. "You good with heights?"

Silas gave a short grin. "I'm good with not staying down here."

"That works," Tarin said.

Darren didn't ask.

He simply stepped into position.

Torlan looked between them.

Then nodded once.

"We go light," he said. "No extra weight. We're not climbing—we're mapping."

Alex stepped in front of them briefly. "Time limit," she said. "We do not get caught in the fog."

"Yes," Torlan said.

She held his gaze a moment longer.

Then stepped back.

"Go."

---

The first section was deceptive.

From below, it had looked manageable—just a series of uneven rises.

Up close, it demanded precision.

Each foothold had to be tested.

Each handhold confirmed.

Loose stone shifted where it shouldn't.

Stable rock sometimes gave under pressure.

Tarin moved slightly ahead, reading the terrain with practiced ease, but not rushing.

"Here," he said, placing his foot onto a narrow shelf. "Weight straight down. Not out."

Silas followed, more carefully than he would have admitted.

"Feels like it's going to slide," he said.

"It won't," Tarin replied. "Unless you push sideways."

"That's comforting."

Darren came next, his movements controlled, efficient. He didn't waste motion. He didn't guess. He watched, then acted.

Torlan moved last.

Not because he needed to.

Because he was watching all of them.

Measuring.

Learning how each one moved.

Where they hesitated.

Where they adjusted.

The ledge narrowed.

Then widened again.

Then angled upward sharply toward a break in the rock that forced them to climb rather than step.

Tarin stopped.

"This is the first choke," he said.

Silas looked up. "That's not a choke," he said. "That's a wall."

"Three meters," Darren said. "Maybe four."

"No clean path," Tarin added.

Torlan stepped forward.

He studied the section.

Then moved.

No hesitation.

He placed one hand high, found a narrow crack, tested it—then shifted his weight upward in a single, controlled motion. His foot found a hold that wasn't obvious from below. His body aligned with the rock.

He moved again.

Higher.

Then again.

Within seconds, he reached the top of the break and turned.

"Stable," he said.

Silas stared up at him. "Well," he muttered, "that looked easier from down here."

Tarin glanced at him. "It always does."

Torlan crouched slightly and extended a hand—not to pull, but to guide.

"Right side," he said. "There's a hold you won't see unless you're looking for it."

Tarin went next.

Then Darren.

Each movement careful.

Measured.

Silas followed last, less smooth—but successful.

At the top, the terrain shifted again.

A wider shelf.

Not comfortable.

But usable.

Torlan stood and looked ahead.

The route continued.

Not straight.

Never straight.

It angled across the face of the canyon wall, disappearing into a tighter section where the rock folded inward, creating shadow and uncertainty.

Darren stepped beside him. "That's where it gets difficult," he said.

"Yes."

"Too narrow in places."

"Yes."

Tarin joined them. "We'll need single file through there," he said. "And no mistakes."

Silas looked back down.

The camp below was already smaller.

Distant.

The boundary stones barely visible.

"That's higher than I expected," he said.

"And not high enough," Torlan replied.

Silas exhaled. "Of course it isn't."

Torlan stepped forward again, moving toward the next section.

This time slower.

More deliberate.

The rock ahead was different.

Less stable.

More fractured.

Tarin moved alongside him. "We don't push past this point," he said quietly.

Torlan paused.

Studied it.

Then nodded.

"Yes," he said.

Darren looked between them. "Why?"

"Because this is where it changes," Tarin said. "Below this, we control movement. Above it—" he shook his head slightly "—the terrain controls us."

Torlan held his gaze.

Then looked ahead once more.

Measured.

Calculated.

And stepped back.

"We return," he said.

Silas blinked. "That's it?"

"For now," Torlan said.

Silas looked ahead again. "Feels like we're stopping early."

"We're stopping correctly," Darren said.

That quieted him.

They turned.

The descent was slower.

More careful.

Each step reversed.

Each hold rechecked.

The margin for error felt thinner on the way down.

But they made it.

When they reached the canyon floor again, the group was waiting.

Not anxiously.

But attentively.

Alex stepped forward. "Well?" she asked.

Torlan looked at the wall.

Then at the group.

"We have a route," he said.

Tarin added, "It's not easy."

Darren finished, "But it works."

Gideon stepped closer. "How long?"

Torlan considered.

"Multiple stages," he said. "We move in sections. Establish positions. No one rushes."

Gideon nodded slowly. "And the choke point?"

"We manage it," Torlan said.

Silas gave a short breath. "That sounds optimistic."

"No," Torlan replied. "It's precise."

Alex looked between them.

Then nodded.

"All right," she said. "We begin staging."

The group moved.

Not uncertain now.

Not hesitant.

They had seen the path.

Not imagined.

Not hoped.

Seen.

Torlan turned once more toward the canyon wall.

The route was there.

Not obvious.

Not forgiving.

But real.

And for the first time—

They had a way forward.

## Chapter 18 - First Movement

They did not take everything.

That was the first decision.

It came quickly.

Without debate.

Torlan stood at the base of the route, looking from the wall… to the group… to the supplies they had gathered.

"We move light first," he said.

Gideon nodded immediately. "Agreed. Establish the first position."

Alex added, "Medical goes in stages. We don't risk the injured on the first pass."

Lena looked at her. "You want me to stay with them?"

"Yes," Alex said. "You and two others. Minimal movement. Keep them stable until we call for transfer."

That settled it.

The structure formed.

Not assigned.

Understood.

The first group assembled near the base.

Torlan.

Tarin.

Darren.

Silas.

Gideon.

Three others chosen for strength and balance.

No excess weight.

Just what they needed to establish the first stage.

Torlan looked at each of them once.

Not for reassurance.

For readiness.

Then he turned.

And began.

The first section climbed faster than it had during scouting.

Not because it was easier.

Because now—

There was no hesitation.

Each movement followed the one before it.

Foot.

Hand.

Shift.

Hold.

Tarin led again, reading the stone with quiet precision. "Left side here," he said. "Better hold."

Gideon followed, steady, controlled. Not fast—but consistent.

Silas came next, quieter now, his earlier edge replaced by concentration.

Darren moved with efficiency, adjusting without wasted motion.

Torlan remained at the rear.

Watching.

Always watching.

The first ledge came into view.

Then beneath them.

Then—

They were on it.

The shelf held.

Not comfortably.

But enough.

Gideon turned, looking down.

The camp was smaller now.

Contained.

"Stage one," he said.

Torlan nodded once.

"Yes."

They didn't stop long.

"Forward," Torlan said.

The choke point came faster than it had during scouting.

It always did.

When movement carried weight.

When consequence followed every step.

The wall rose in front of them again.

Three meters.

Maybe four.

No clear path.

Tarin moved first.

Same holds.

Same sequence.

Up.

Across.

Over.

Gideon followed.

Then Darren.

Each one slower now.

More deliberate.

The margin had narrowed.

Silas reached the base of the wall and looked up. "Still not a fan of this part," he said.

"No one is," Darren replied.

Silas exhaled.

Then climbed.

Torlan waited until all of them had cleared.

Then stepped forward.

He didn't climb the way they had.

He moved through it.

One motion.

Then another.

Not rushed.

Not forced.

But with a strength that removed hesitation.

He reached the top and turned.

Silas shook his head slightly. "I'm not even going to comment on that."

Torlan didn't respond.

He was already looking ahead.

The next section changed everything.

The ledge narrowed.

Not gradually.

Immediately.

A foot wide.

Then less.

The wall pressed inward on one side.

The drop opened on the other.

Tarin stopped.

"This is it," he said.

Gideon stepped up beside him. "Single file," he said.

"Yes."

"No loose movement."

"No."

They all understood.

Tarin went first.

One step.

Pause.

Test.

Then another.

The rock held.

Barely.

Gideon followed.

Then Darren.

Then Silas.

Each step placed with care.

Each movement controlled.

No wasted motion.

No distraction.

Halfway across—

A stone shifted.

Small.

But enough.

Silas froze.

"Don't move," Gideon said quietly.

"I'm not," Silas replied.

Torlan stepped closer.

Not onto the ledge.

Close enough.

"Weight forward," he said.

Silas adjusted.

Slowly.

The rock settled.

Held.

"Continue," Torlan said.

Silas moved.

Carefully.

Deliberately.

And cleared the section.

One by one, they crossed.

Until Torlan remained.

He stepped onto the narrow ledge.

Tested it once.

Then moved.

Not cautiously.

Not recklessly.

Precisely.

The rock held.

As if it had decided to.

He crossed.

And stepped onto stable ground.

They stood there for a moment.

Not resting.

Just—

Acknowledging.

They had passed the first real barrier.

Gideon looked ahead. "How far to the next stage?"

Torlan scanned the wall.

Measured.

"Another thirty meters," he said. "Then a wider shelf."

Gideon nodded. "We establish there."

"Yes."

They moved again.

Slower now.

The fatigue had begun.

Not sharp.

Not immediate.

But present.

Each step carried more weight.

Each hold required more attention.

When they reached the next shelf, it was wider.

Safer.

Enough to stand without thinking about it.

Gideon exhaled. "This works."

Torlan nodded once.

"Yes."

He turned.

Looked back down.

The camp below was distant now.

Partially obscured by the returning fog.

Already rising.

Even in daylight.

Tarin followed his gaze. "We made the right call," he said.

"Yes," Torlan replied.

Gideon stepped forward. "We mark this as Stage One," he said. "We bring the next group."

Alex's voice came faintly from below.

Not distorted.

Not lost.

But thinner than it should have been.

"We're ready!"

Torlan listened.

Measured the delay.

Still present.

Still wrong.

But better.

He looked at the group.

Then back down.

"We bring them up," he said.

Silas sat briefly, wiping his hands against his pants. "You know," he said, "I'm starting to appreciate the idea of being somewhere else."

Darren gave a slight nod. "That's the plan."

Torlan didn't sit.

He remained standing.

Watching the route.

Watching the fog.

Watching the timing.

Below them, the next group began to move.

Above them, the wall continued.

And for the first time—

They were partway out.

## Chapter 19 - The Carry

They did not bring the injured up all at once.

That was the second decision.

As important as the first.

Torlan stood at the edge of the Stage One shelf, looking down at the canyon floor where the next group had begun assembling. The fog was already returning along the lowest ground, rising in thin layers that would thicken as the day wore on.

Time was narrowing again.

"We rotate," Gideon said beside him. "No one carries the full distance alone."

Torlan nodded once. "Yes."

Alex's voice came up from below—clear, but thinner than it should have been.

"First stretcher ready!"

Torlan measured the delay.

Still present.

Still wrong.

But manageable.

"Send them," he called.

The first stretcher moved slowly.

Four carriers.

Two on each side.

Improvised from the support panels and reinforced straps they had salvaged from the shuttle.

The injured man lay secured across it, conscious, but pale.

Alex moved beside them, guiding.

"Keep it level," she said. "No sudden shifts. Let the front set the pace."

They reached the base of the first incline.

Stopped.

Adjusted.

Then began the climb.

From above, the movement looked controlled.

From within it—

It was effort.

Every step required agreement.

The front pair had to move first.

The rear had to match.

Too fast, and the stretcher tilted.

Too slow, and the weight dragged.

Tarin moved ahead of them, calling out placements.

"Left foot there—no, not that one—the darker rock."

The front carrier adjusted.

The stretcher steadied.

They moved again.

Halfway up the first section, the strain began to show.

One of the rear carriers faltered slightly.

Not a stumble.

Just enough.

"Hold," Alex said immediately.

They stopped.

Carefully.

The injured man drew in a sharp breath.

"Sorry," the carrier said.

"You're fine," Alex replied. "We adjust."

Torlan stepped down from the ledge.

Not all the way.

Just enough.

"Switch," he said.

The carrier hesitated. "I can—"

"Switch," Torlan repeated.

No force.

No argument.

The man nodded.

Stepped back.

Torlan took position.

One hand under the frame.

Lifted.

The weight changed.

Not reduced.

Redistributed.

The stretcher steadied.

Alex watched him for a moment.

Then nodded once.

"Move."

They reached the first ledge.

Set the stretcher down carefully.

No one spoke for a few seconds.

Not because they didn't want to.

Because they needed the breath.

Silas leaned back slightly, flexing his hands. "That," he said quietly, "is heavier than it looks."

Darren glanced at him. "Everything is."

Torlan didn't rest long.

He looked ahead.

Then back.

"Next section," he said.

The climb to the choke point was slower.

Not because the path had changed.

Because the load had.

The stretcher extended beyond the width of the narrow sections.

That changed everything.

Tarin stopped before the choke.

"This won't fit clean," he said.

Gideon stepped forward. "We angle it," he said. "Front lifts. Rear lowers."

Alex shook her head. "Too much tilt."

"Then we rotate carriers across the choke," Gideon said.

Torlan looked at the section.

Measured.

Then nodded.

"Yes."

They set the stretcher down again.

Carefully.

The fog below had risen higher now.

The camp was no longer fully visible.

Only shapes.

Movement without detail.

"Front two go first," Gideon said. "Then we pass the stretcher across. One side at a time."

Alex looked at the injured man. "You'll feel movement," she said. "Stay as still as you can."

He nodded.

Didn't speak.

The first pair crossed.

Slow.

Precise.

No mistakes.

They reached the other side.

Turned.

Ready.

"Lift," Torlan said.

The stretcher rose.

Angled.

Not level.

But controlled.

Darren moved first, guiding the front edge across the narrow section.

One step.

Pause.

Adjust.

Then another.

The rock shifted.

Slight.

But enough.

Darren froze.

"Hold," Torlan said.

Everything stopped.

The stretcher hung between two positions.

Not stable.

Not falling.

Waiting.

Silas exhaled slowly. "This is not my favorite moment."

"No one asked you," Gideon said quietly.

Torlan shifted his grip.

Not forcefully.

Carefully.

He adjusted the angle.

Reduced the strain on the unstable edge.

"Now," he said.

Darren moved.

One step.

Then another.

The stretcher cleared the narrowest point.

The front pair took the weight.

Stabilized.

"Rear," Torlan said.

The remaining carriers crossed.

One by one.

Then—

He followed.

Last.

They set the stretcher down on the far side.

Fully.

Securely.

Alex checked immediately.

Pulse.

Breathing.

Stability.

"He's holding," she said.

The group exhaled.

Not relief.

Not yet.

But progress.

They reached Stage One.

Placed the injured along the inner edge where the rock offered the most protection.

Lena, who had come up with the second group, moved into position immediately.

"I've got him," she said.

Alex nodded. "Keep him warm. Minimal movement."

Torlan stood.

Looked down.

The fog had risen further.

The canyon floor was now a blur of shifting gray.

Only the immediate base of the climb remained visible.

Not for long.

Gideon stepped beside him. "We won't get everyone up in one pass."

"No," Torlan said.

"We stage."

"Yes."

Gideon nodded slowly. "Then we keep moving."

Silas sat back again, shaking his head slightly. "You know," he said, "this is about the point where I'd normally reconsider my life choices."

Darren gave a small, almost absent nod. "You still can."

Silas looked at him.

Then down at the fog.

Then back up.

"No," he said. "I don't think I can."

Torlan didn't respond.

He was already looking at the next group below.

Already measuring the time.

Already planning the next movement.

Behind them, the first of the injured had made it up.

Ahead of them, the wall still rose.

And below—

The canyon was beginning to disappear.

# Chapter 20 - The Narrow Pass

They did not wait.

That was the third decision.

Not because they had strength to spare.

Because they did not.

But because the fog was already rising again.

Faster.

Earlier.

Less forgiving.

Torlan stood at the edge of Stage One, watching the next group form below through a thinning gap in the fog. The canyon floor was already beginning to blur at its edges, the lower ground softening into gray that would soon become obstruction.

"We take the next stretcher now," Gideon said.

Torlan nodded. "Yes."

Alex's voice came up from below. "Second ready!"

Torlan measured the delay.

Still there.

Still wrong.

But enough.

"Send them," he called.

The second carry was harder.

Not because the path had changed.

Because fatigue had.

The carriers moved with less reserve now. The rhythm took longer to establish. The first incline felt steeper, though it wasn't. Hands searched longer for holds they had already used once before.

"Slow," Alex said. "Match the front."

They did.

Because they had to.

At Stage One, the rotation was faster.

No wasted time.

Darren stepped in before being asked.

Silas didn't argue.

Gideon took the rear.

Torlan took the front left.

The weight lifted.

Shifted.

Settled.

"Move," Torlan said.

The approach to the choke point felt tighter this time.

Not physically.

Mentally.

Everyone knew what was coming.

No one said it.

Tarin reached the edge first and stopped.

The narrow pass stretched ahead—less a ledge than a compromise between wall and drop. The rock pressed inward on one side, forcing bodies toward the open air on the other. The path angled slightly upward, just enough to make footing uncertain under load.

"It's worse with weight," Tarin said.

"Yes," Torlan replied.

Gideon stepped beside him. "Same method?"

Torlan studied the stone.

The fractures.

The places where the rock would hold—and where it would not.

Then nodded.

"Yes."

They set the stretcher down just before the pass.

Carefully.

No one spoke for a moment.

Not from hesitation.

From focus.

Alex crouched beside the injured woman on the stretcher. "You'll feel the tilt again," she said quietly. "Stay with us."

The woman nodded, her eyes closed, her breathing shallow but controlled.

"We'll get you across," Alex added.

Then she stood.

"Front goes first," Gideon said.

Tarin and Darren moved.

One step onto the ledge.

Then another.

They reached the far side and turned.

Ready.

"Lift," Torlan said.

The stretcher rose.

Angled.

More sharply this time.

The front dipped slightly as Darren adjusted.

"Higher," Tarin said. "Bring it up."

Torlan shifted.

The frame rose.

Stabilized.

"Move," he said.

Darren stepped onto the ledge.

The stretcher extended past the safe line.

The margin disappeared.

One step.

Pause.

Another.

The rock held.

Then—

Didn't.

A section of stone under Darren's forward foot broke loose.

Not large.

But enough.

His foot dropped.

The stretcher dipped sharply.

The woman gasped.

"Hold!" Gideon snapped.

Everything froze.

The stretcher hung at an angle.

Front low.

Rear high.

Weight pulling sideways.

The narrow ledge suddenly smaller than it had been seconds before.

Darren didn't speak.

He adjusted.

Not upward.

Inward.

Pressing his body against the rock.

Reducing the outward pull.

"Don't correct fast," Torlan said.

Darren nodded once.

"On your word," he said.

Torlan shifted his position.

Not stepping onto the ledge.

Not yet.

He moved closer.

Close enough to change the geometry.

"Bring it to me," he said.

Gideon glanced at him. "That's a reach."

"Yes."

"It'll shift the load."

"Yes."

A moment.

Then—

"Do it," Gideon said.

Darren moved.

One inch.

Then another.

The stretcher shifted.

Torlan stepped onto the ledge.

One foot.

Then the other.

No hesitation.

No wasted motion.

He reached.

Took the forward corner.

Lifted.

Not abruptly.

Completely.

The weight transferred.

The tilt reduced.

The stretcher leveled.

"Now," Torlan said.

Darren moved.

Cleared the unstable section.

Tarin took the front again.

Stabilized.

"Rear," Gideon said.

Silas and the remaining carrier crossed.

Carefully.

No slip.

No hesitation.

Torlan remained last.

Still holding the forward corner.

Still on the narrowest part of the ledge.

He waited until the path was clear.

Then moved.

Not slowly.

Not quickly.

Precisely.

Each step placed.

Each hold chosen.

He crossed.

And stepped onto solid ground.

The stretcher came down.

Fully.

Securely.

Alex moved in immediately.

"Stay with me," she said.

Pulse.

Breathing.

She nodded.

"She's stable."

No one spoke for a moment.

The silence was not relief.

Not yet.

It was recalibration.

Silas let out a breath. "That," he said, "was worse."

Darren gave a small nod. "Yes."

Gideon looked back at the pass.

The broken section of rock was visible now.

A gap where footing had been.

"That's not holding for the next group," he said.

Torlan followed his gaze.

"No," he said.

Tarin stepped closer. "We adjust the line," he said. "Higher on entry. Shift left earlier."

Gideon nodded. "We mark it."

"Yes."

Below them, the fog had risen further.

The canyon floor was gone now.

Completely.

Only the lower section of the climb remained visible—and that was fading.

"We don't have time for mistakes," Gideon said.

"No," Torlan replied.

He looked ahead.

The next section rose again.

Not as narrow.

But steeper.

More exposed.

Behind them, the second injured had crossed.

Ahead of them, the path continued.

And the margin—
Was getting thinner.

## Chapter 21 - Forced Pause

They didn't plan to stop.

That was the problem.

The plan had been movement.

Continuous.

Measured—but uninterrupted.

The wall had other ideas.

The next section rose sharply from the far side of the narrow pass, angling upward along a fractured face that offered holds—but not easily, and not in a way that favored a group moving under load.

The third stretcher had just cleared the choke point when it began.

Not a fall.

Not a slip.

A slowdown.

Small at first.

Then undeniable.

"Hold," Alex said.

The word came quickly.

Not loud.

But final.

The stretcher stopped.

Carriers locked in place.

Breathing heavy.

"What is it?" Gideon asked.

Alex was already moving.

She reached the stretcher, her hands steady despite the incline.
The injured man—one of the earlier critical cases—had gone pale.
Not from the climb.
From within.
"Stay with me," she said.
His eyes opened slightly.
Not focused.
Not fully there.
Torlan stepped closer.
"What changed?" he asked.
Alex didn't look up.
"He's dropping," she said.
"How far?"
"Too fast."

The rock beneath them shifted slightly as one of the carriers adjusted position.
"Don't move," Torlan said.
The man froze.

Gideon looked ahead.
Then back.
"We can't hold here," he said.
"No," Alex agreed.
"But we can't move him like this."

That was the point.
The place where the plan met reality.
And stopped.

The fog below had risen past the narrow pass now.
The canyon floor was gone.
The route behind them—half visible.
The route ahead—uncertain.

The group stretched along the wall.
Exposed.
Committed.

"We take him up," Silas said.
Alex shook her head. "Not like this."
"We don't have a choice."
"We do," she said.
Gideon stepped in. "What choice?"
Alex looked at him.
"We stabilize," she said.
"Here?" Gideon asked.
"Yes."
He glanced around.
The incline.
The limited space.
The drop.
"This isn't a place to stop."
"No," Alex said.
"But it's where we are."

Silence.
Not agreement.
Recognition.

Torlan looked ahead.
Measured the distance to the next shelf.
Then looked back.
Measured the group.
Then down.
Measured the fog.
Everything moved.
Everything changed.

Except one thing.

The condition of the man on the stretcher.

"We pause," Torlan said.

Gideon turned. "For how long?"

"Long enough," Torlan replied.

"For what?"

"For him," Torlan said.

Gideon held his gaze.

Then looked at the man.

Then back at the wall.

Then nodded.

"Stage hold," he said.

The group adjusted.

Not comfortably.

Not easily.

But deliberately.

They shifted the stretcher.

Carefully.

Angling it toward a slight indentation in the rock—a place where the wall pressed inward just enough to offer minimal support.

Not safe.

Less unsafe.

"Lower," Alex said.

"Slow."

The stretcher came down.

Not flat.

But stable enough.

Lena moved in beside her.

"What do you need?" she asked.

"Water," Alex said. "Minimal. Keep him conscious."

Darren stepped back slightly, scanning the line of people along the wall.

"We're stacked too tight," he said.

"Yes," Torlan replied.

"We need separation."

"Yes."

Gideon took over.

"You—back five meters," he said, pointing.

"Find stable footing. No crowding."

The group obeyed.

Not because of rank.

Because it made sense.

Silas leaned back against the rock, breathing hard. "This is the part they don't show you," he muttered.

"What part?" Tarin asked.

"The part where you stop and realize you're not in control of how fast this goes."

Tarin gave a small nod.

"No," he said. "You're not."

Torlan remained standing.

He didn't sit.

Didn't lean.

He watched.

The man on the stretcher.

The group.

The wall.

The fog.

Alex worked.

Quietly.

Precisely.

Every movement intentional.
No wasted motion.
No panic.

Minutes passed.
Longer than they should have.
Shorter than they needed.

The man's breathing steadied.
Not strong.
But not dropping.
Alex exhaled slowly.
"He's holding," she said.

Gideon looked at Torlan. "Can he move?"
Torlan didn't answer.
He looked at Alex.
She met his gaze.
Then nodded once.
"Yes," she said.
"Carefully."

Torlan stepped forward.
"We move again," he said.

No one argued.
Not this time.

The group re-formed.
More spread out.
More aware.
Less confident.
But stronger.

"Rotation every ten meters," Gideon said.
"Call it early," Alex added.
"No delays."

They lifted.

The stretcher rose.

Settled.

Torlan moved to the front.

This time—

He didn't stay back.

"Follow my steps," he said.

They moved.

Slower.

More deliberate.

Each step chosen.

Each hold confirmed.

The wall did not become easier.

But the group became better.

Below them, the fog continued to rise.

Above them, the next shelf waited.

And for the first time since the climb began—

They understood something clearly.

This was not about reaching the top quickly.

This was about reaching it at all.

## Chapter 22 - Ledge Camp

They did not reach the next shelf before the light began to fail. That was the fourth decision.

Not spoken.

Recognized.

Torlan saw it first.

Not in the sky.

In the wall.

The holds were becoming harder to read.

The shadows deeper.

The margin thinner.

He stopped.

"Hold," he said.

The word moved through the line.

Passed back.

Carried forward.

Until the entire group stilled along the rock face.

Gideon stepped up beside him. "We're close," he said.

Torlan nodded.

"Yes."

"How far?"

"Less than twenty meters."

Gideon exhaled. "We can make that."

Torlan didn't answer immediately.

He looked at the rock ahead.

Then at the group behind.

Then down.

The fog had risen again.

Higher than before.

Faster.

The lower sections of the climb were already gone.

Completely.

"We stop here," Torlan said.

Gideon looked at him.

Not disagreement.

Evaluation.

Then he followed Torlan's gaze.

Saw the same thing.

And nodded.

"Ledge hold," he said.

The adjustment began.

Not easy.

Not comfortable.

But necessary.

The section they had reached was not a true shelf.

It was a widening.

A place where the wall pressed inward just enough to allow partial footing and partial support.

Not flat.

Not safe.

But survivable.

"Set the stretchers first," Alex said.

"Inner side. Close to the wall."

The carriers shifted.

Carefully.

Lowered the injured into position.

Each movement measured.

Each adjustment deliberate.

Lena moved immediately into place beside them.

"I've got them," she said.

Alex nodded once.

"Rotate watch on breathing," she said. "No one drifts."

Silas leaned back against the rock and let out a slow breath.

"This is what we're calling camp now?"

Tarin glanced at him. "For tonight," he said.

Silas looked down.

There was nothing to see.

Only fog.

Dense.

Unbroken.

The canyon had disappeared.

"I preferred it when I could see how far down it was," Silas muttered.

"No," Darren said quietly. "You didn't."

Silas considered that.

Then nodded.

"No," he said. "I didn't."

Gideon moved along the line, adjusting positions.

"Spacing," he said. "No one crowds. Keep three points of contact if you're standing."

People shifted.

Not far.

Just enough.

Torlan remained near the outer edge.

Not at risk.

Not exposed.

Just—

Present.

Watching.

The light faded further.

The strip of sky above narrowed.

Then dimmed.

Then softened into something that no longer defined time.

The fog rose again.

But differently.

Not around them.

Below them.

It filled the canyon like water.

Layer upon layer.

Until there was no sense of depth at all.

Only distance removed.

Alex stepped closer to Torlan.

"It's different up here," she said.

"Yes."

"Less distortion."

"Yes."

She listened.

The canyon was not silent.

But the sound had changed.

The strange shifting of direction was gone.

What remained—

Was distance.

Then—

A sound.

Low.

Far below.

A growl.

Faint.

But real.

Silas stiffened slightly. "They're still there."

"Yes," Tarin said.

"They followed."

"No," Torlan replied.

"They remained."

Another sound.

From deeper in the canyon.

Not circling.

Not testing.

Moving.

But not toward them.

Gideon looked down into the fog.

"They're not climbing," he said.

"No," Torlan said.

"Why not?"

Torlan didn't answer immediately.

Then—

"The terrain favors them below," he said.

"And not here."

That settled something.

Not completely.

But enough.

The group adjusted again.

More quietly now.

Less tension.

Not safe.

But less threatened.

Lena checked one of the injured.

"Breathing's steady," she said.

Alex nodded.

"Keep them warm."

Darren sat for the first time since the climb had begun.

Not fully relaxed.

But no longer standing.

Silas followed.

Carefully.

Testing his footing before committing weight.

Gideon remained standing a while longer.

Then finally lowered himself against the rock.

Not because he wanted to.

Because he needed to.

Torlan did not sit.

Not yet.

He watched the line.

The spacing.

The holds.

The fog.

The sky.

Alex looked at him.

"You should rest," she said.

He shook his head once.

"Later."

She didn't argue.

Time passed.

Not measured.

Felt.

The group grew quieter.

Movement reduced.

Breathing slowed.

The fear from the canyon floor did not follow them fully.

But it had changed them.

That remained.

After a while, Gideon spoke.

Not loudly.

Not to command.

To acknowledge.

"We hold here," he said.

No one responded.

They didn't need to.

Torlan finally shifted.

Lowered himself onto a narrow section of rock.

Not fully seated.

But supported.

Alex sat beside him.

Close.

Not touching.

Below them, the canyon was gone.

Above them, the path remained.

For the first time since the crash—

They were not surrounded.

They were on the way out.

## Chapter 23 - Final Push

They began before the light.

Not because they could see clearly.

Because they understood the timing.

Torlan was already awake when the first faint shift in the sky began—a subtle lightening along the narrow strip above them that marked the beginning of the window.

He stood without sound.

Checked the line.

The spacing.

The holds.

Nothing had changed.

Except the opportunity.

"Up," he said quietly.

The word moved through the group.

Soft.

Controlled.

Immediate.

Alex was already moving.

Checking the injured.

"Wake them gently," she said to Lena. "No sudden movement."

Lena nodded.

The group stirred.

Not slowly.

Not reluctantly.
With purpose.

Gideon rose, stretching once, then stopping himself before shifting his balance too far. "We move in five," he said.
Torlan nodded.
"Yes."

The fog below had not lifted yet.
But it had thinned.
Enough.
The canyon still existed.
But not clearly.
That was all they needed.

"Rotation stays tight," Alex said. "No overextension."
Gideon added, "Call fatigue early. No one pushes past their limit."
Silas gave a quiet breath. "That's new."
"No," Gideon said. "That's necessary."

They lifted.
The stretcher rose.
Settled.
This time—
More controlled.
Less hesitation.

Torlan moved to the front.
Not watching.
Leading.

"Follow my steps," he said.

The wall rose immediately.
Steeper than before.
Less forgiving.
The holds were there—

But farther apart.
Less obvious.

Torlan climbed.
Not testing.
Knowing.
Each placement exact.
Each movement efficient.
No wasted motion.

Behind him, the group followed.
Not matching his pace.
Matching his pattern.

Tarin moved just behind.
Calling adjustments.
"Right side—no, higher."
"Shift weight inward."
"Don't trust that edge."

The stretcher came next.
Lifted.
Angled.
Carried.

Silas grunted. "This is getting vertical."
"It is vertical," Darren said.

Halfway up the section—
One of the carriers slowed.
"Switch," Gideon said immediately.
They adjusted.
Smooth.
No delay.
The stretcher remained level.

Alex moved alongside.

"Stay with me," she said to the injured.

A faint nod.

Still conscious.

Still holding.

The wall pressed in.

Then opened.

Then pressed again.

Each change requiring adjustment.

Each adjustment requiring attention.

Torlan reached the final break.

The last rise before the shelf.

He paused.

Measured.

Then moved.

This section was different.

Not narrow.

Not unstable.

Demanding.

The holds were fewer.

The distance greater.

Strength mattered here.

Torlan climbed.

One motion.

Then another.

His hand found a hold others would have missed.

His foot set against a surface that should not have supported weight—

But did.

He reached the top.

Turned.

"Up," he said.

Tarin followed.

Then Darren.

Each one working harder now.

Each movement requiring more effort.

Silas reached the final section and looked up. "You've got to be kidding me."

"No," Gideon said. "We don't."

Silas exhaled.

Then climbed.

The stretcher came last.

This was the hardest part.

The angle.

The distance.

The lack of stable footing.

"We lift higher," Torlan said.

"Full extension."

Gideon nodded. "Do it."

They raised the stretcher.

Higher than before.

Almost overhead.

"Move," Torlan said.

Darren stepped first.

Then Tarin.

They took the front weight.

Pulled.

Not sharply.

Steadily.

The stretcher rose.

Slow.

Controlled.

The rear carriers pushed upward.

Every movement aligned.

Every motion deliberate.

The final edge came.

Close.

Then closer.

Then—

Reached.

Torlan stepped forward.

Took the frame.

Lifted.

Not just enough.

All the way.

The stretcher cleared the edge.

"Set," he said.

They lowered it.

Carefully.

Securely.

Alex moved in immediately.

"He's stable," she said.

The others followed.

One by one.

Climbing.

Reaching.

Crossing.

Silas pulled himself over the edge and lay back for a second. "I'm going to pretend that was easier than it felt."

"No one will believe you," Darren said.

Gideon stepped onto the shelf.

Turned.

Looked back.

The canyon below was gone.

Not hidden.

Gone.

Filled completely with fog.

A solid field of gray that erased depth, erased distance, erased everything they had left behind.

"We're above it," he said.

Torlan stepped onto the shelf.

Fully.

For the first time.

He turned.

Looked out.

The space ahead opened.

Not wide.

But wider.

The air clearer.

The light stronger.

Alex stood beside him.

"It's different," she said.

"Yes."

Behind them, the group gathered.

Not tightly.

Not out of fear.

Because they could.

Lena adjusted the injured.

Silas sat.

Darren stood.

Tarin scanned ahead.

Gideon exhaled slowly.

Torlan looked forward.

Then back once more.

The canyon remained below.

Unchanged.

Unforgiving.

But they were no longer inside it.

They had crossed.

And for the first time since the crash—

They had reached ground that did not hold them in place.

They had reached the plateau.

## Chapter 24 - The Plateau

They did not celebrate.

That surprised some of them.

After the climb… after the strain… after the narrow pass and the ledge and the long, controlled push through fatigue—

There was no moment of release.

No sudden relief.

Just—

Breathing.

Standing.

Looking.

The plateau stretched ahead in uneven layers of rock and sparse growth, broken by shallow rises and scattered formations that cast longer shadows in the clearer light. It was not smooth ground. It was not easy ground.

But it was open.

That was enough.

Alex moved first.

Not forward.

Back.

Toward the injured.

"Set them here," she said. "This surface is better."

They lowered the stretchers carefully onto a flatter section of rock. Not comfortable—but stable. Lena was already beside her, checking, adjusting, ensuring nothing from the climb had shifted or worsened.

"He made it," Lena said quietly.

Alex nodded once. "Yes."

That mattered.

Gideon stepped out a few paces from the group, scanning the terrain. He turned slowly, taking in distance—real distance—for the first time since the crash.

"I can see," he said.

No one responded.

They understood.

Silas stood beside him after a moment, hands resting on his hips.

"I forgot what that feels like," he said.

"To see where you are," Gideon replied.

"And where you're not," Silas added.

Behind them, Darren had already moved toward a slightly higher point along the plateau's edge. Not far—but enough to gain perspective. He didn't speak. He didn't call anyone over.

He simply looked.

Measured.

Tarin joined him.

"You thinking what I'm thinking?" Tarin asked.

Darren nodded slightly. "Signal might hold here."

"Yes."

"Not perfect," Darren added.

"No," Tarin agreed. "But better."

Torlan stood at the edge of the rise, looking out across the plateau.

The air felt different.

Not lighter.

Clearer.

The distortion that had shaped every sound and every decision in the canyon had loosened its hold. The wind moved more naturally here, carrying scent and sound without bending them out of place.

It changed everything.

Alex stepped up beside him.

"We can breathe," she said.

"Yes."

She looked out across the terrain. "We're not done."

"No."

Behind them, the group had begun to settle.

Not collapsing.

Not resting fully.

But no longer braced against immediate threat.

The difference was subtle.

But real.

Gideon approached.

"We need to secure this position," he said.

Torlan nodded once.

"Yes."

"Perimeter first," Gideon continued. "Then signal. Then next move."

Alex glanced at him.

No resistance.

No argument.

Just alignment.

Silas looked between them. "You two are getting along better," he said.

Gideon didn't respond.

Torlan didn't either.

They didn't need to.

Darren stepped back down from the rise. "We should test signal while the window holds," he said.

Torlan looked at him.

"Yes."

Darren gave a slight nod.

Not seeking approval.

Not avoiding it.

Simply part of the structure now.

Alex turned. "Set up here," she said to Lena. "Keep them stable. Call if anything changes."

Lena nodded. "I've got them."

Tarin moved outward, scanning the terrain for natural boundaries—places where the ground dipped or rose just enough to define a safer edge.

Silas followed, slower now, more deliberate.

Gideon began assigning positions.

No one questioned him.

Torlan stepped toward the signal unit as Darren began assembling it again.

The components were the same.

The environment was not.

"Power first," Darren said.

Torlan nodded.

Alex joined them.

"Let's see if it holds," she said.

The unit came alive.

Not flickering.

Not struggling.

Stable.

Darren adjusted the alignment.

"Better," he said.

Torlan watched the readout.

The delay—

Reduced.

Not gone.

But manageable.

Alex looked at him. "Now?"

"Yes."

Fredrick's absence was felt again.

This would have been his moment.

His voice.

His call.

Alex picked up the receiver.

No hesitation.

"Outpost Meridian," she said. "This is Alex Hale. Emergency transmission from downed shuttle. Do you copy?"

The signal went out.

Clean.

Clear.

Held.

For a moment—

Nothing.

Then—

"…Hale…reading you…signal stable…repeat—signal stable…"

Alex's eyes lifted.

She didn't smile.

But something in her changed.

"We copy," she said. "Twenty-three survivors. Multiple injuries. We are on elevated ground—signal holding."

The response came back.

Clearer.

Stronger.

"…confirm…rescue en route…provide coordinates…"

Darren glanced at Torlan.

Torlan nodded.

Darren entered the data.

Precise.

Measured.

"Coordinates transmitting," Alex said.

The signal held.

No fragmentation.

No delay that broke meaning.

"…received…stay in position…ETA—unknown…search pattern expanding…"

Alex lowered the receiver slowly.

Looked at Torlan.

"They've got us," she said.

Torlan nodded once.

"Yes."

Behind them, the group had gone quiet.

Not from fear.

From understanding.

Gideon stepped closer. "They heard?"

"Yes."

He exhaled.

Slow.

Controlled.

Silas looked out across the plateau. "Well," he said, "I'd say that was worth the climb."

No one disagreed.

Torlan turned once more toward the canyon.

The fog still filled it.

Unchanged.

Unmoved.

But it no longer held them.

He looked forward again.

Across the plateau.

Toward whatever came next.

They had survived the canyon.

Now—

They had to survive the rest.

## Chapter 25 - Establishing the Plateau

They did not move far from where they had come up.

That was the first decision on the plateau.

Not because there weren't better places.

Because they had already paid the cost to reach this one.

Torlan stood at the edge of the rise, looking outward across the broken stretch of ground ahead. The plateau wasn't flat—not truly. It rolled in shallow ridges and uneven shelves, dotted with low growth and scattered stone that offered both cover and complication.

But this position—

It had advantages.

Visibility.

Access to the climb route.

Stable ground beneath their feet.

Enough space to organize.

"That's our center," Gideon said, stepping up beside him.

Torlan nodded once.

"Yes."

The group began to move.

Not scattered.

Directed.

"Perimeter first," Gideon called. "Mark a boundary—visible and physical."

Silas picked up a loose stone and set it down several meters out.
"Like the canyon," he said.
"Better than the canyon," Gideon replied.
Tarin moved farther out, identifying natural breaks in the terrain—low ridges where the ground dipped just enough to define an edge.
"Use the land," he said. "Don't fight it."
Darren followed, adjusting placements where stones alone wouldn't hold meaning from a distance.
Within minutes, the shape of a camp began to form.
Not tight.
Not defensive.
But structured.

Alex focused on the injured.
"Here," she said, directing Lena and two others to a slightly recessed section of rock that offered minimal wind protection.
They lowered the stretchers carefully.
"Keep them shaded as much as possible," Alex said. "We rotate positions with the sun."
Lena nodded. "Water?"
"Small amounts," Alex replied. "Controlled."

The reality of the plateau began to settle in.
The air was clearer.
But harsher.
The light stronger.
The wind more consistent.
There was no canyon wall to shield them now.
No enclosure.

Silas looked around, squinting slightly. "Feels like we traded one problem for another."
Darren glanced at him. "We traded a trap for exposure."

Silas considered that.

Then nodded.

"I'll take exposure."

Torlan turned toward the equipment.

"Signal," he said.

Darren was already moving.

The unit came together quickly.

Faster than before.

Not because the equipment had changed.

Because the environment had.

"Power stable," Darren said.

Torlan watched the readout.

The delay was still there.

But reduced.

Contained.

Alex stepped in beside them.

"Let's confirm again," she said.

The signal went out.

Clean.

"Outpost Meridian, this is Hale. Signal holding. Confirm status."

The response came faster this time.

Stronger.

"…Hale…reading clear…rescue team mobilized…ground units deploying…air support active…"

Gideon stepped closer.

"How long?" he asked quietly.

Alex listened.

Then answered.

"Two to three days."

Silas let out a low breath. "That's longer than I was hoping."

"No," Darren said. "It's faster than we should expect."

Torlan looked out across the plateau.

Two to three days.

That meant—

They had time.

And not enough of it.

"Visual signal," he said.

Gideon nodded. "Agreed."

They moved quickly.

The rock "X" took shape first.

Large.

Deliberate.

Visible from above.

Each stone placed with intention—not random, not rushed.

Tarin adjusted the angles. "Make it clean," he said. "Not a pile—a mark."

Next came reflective material.

Panels from the shuttle.

Positioned to catch light.

Darren adjusted alignment twice.

"Better this way," he said. "Sun angle shifts mid-day."

Then—

Fire.

Silas gathered what little combustible material they had salvaged.

Sparse.

Dry.

Not ideal.

"We'll need to conserve it," Alex said.

Silas nodded. "Then we don't light it until we need it."

Torlan looked at the setup.
Then at the sky.
Then at the ground.

"We light only on confirmation," he said.

Gideon nodded. "Agreed."

The structure of the camp settled.
Not complete.
But functional.

Water was counted.
Measured.
Distributed.
Not freely.

Food was rationed.
Strictly.

Positions were assigned.
Not as roles.
As responsibilities.

The group adjusted.
Not easily.
But willingly.

Darren moved along the edge of the perimeter, checking sightlines.
Silas followed, quieter now.
Tarin scanned outward, mapping terrain beyond the immediate camp.

Gideon stood near the center, watching everything.
Not directing constantly.
Just—
Present.

Alex checked the injured again.
"Stable," she said quietly.

Lena nodded.

"For now."

Torlan stood at the edge of the rise.

Looking out.

The plateau stretched ahead.

Open.

Uncertain.

Behind them, the canyon remained.

Hidden beneath the fog.

Still there.

Still dangerous.

But no longer holding them.

Alex stepped beside him.

"We hold here," she said.

"Yes."

She looked out across the terrain.

"Two to three days," she added.

Torlan nodded once.

"Then we make it two to three days," he said.

Behind them, the camp held.

Not comfortably.

But together.

Above them, the sky remained clear.

For now.

And for the first time since reaching the plateau—

They were not just surviving.

They were waiting.

And that required a different kind of strength.

## Chapter 26 - Signal Refinement

The signal held.

That was the first change.

Not perfectly.

Not without variation.

But it held long enough to matter.

Darren adjusted the unit again.

Small movements.

Fractional.

"Angle matters," he said. "Even here."

Torlan stood beside him, watching the readout.

The delay remained.

Reduced.

Not gone.

"Compensate," Torlan said.

Darren nodded. "Already am."

Alex stepped in with the receiver.

"Outpost Meridian, this is Hale. Confirm signal stability on your end."

The response came quickly.

"...Hale...reading consistent...minor distortion...within acceptable range..."

Gideon exhaled slightly. "Good enough," he said.

"Yes," Torlan replied.

Alex continued. "Request update on ground team."

A brief pause.

Then—

"...ground units en route...terrain slowing progress...air reconnaissance active..."

Silas glanced up at the sky. "Haven't seen anything yet."

"You will," Tarin said.

The signal crackled once.

Then steadied again.

"...recommend maintain visual markers...confirm visibility of signal 'X'..."

Darren looked toward the rock formation.

"It's there," he said. "Clean lines."

Torlan nodded. "Confirm."

Alex spoke again. "Marker in place. Reflective panels aligned. Fire ready on request."

"...acknowledged...stand by for aerial pass..."

The signal dropped.

Not lost.

Paused.

Alex lowered the receiver.

"They'll sweep," she said.

Gideon nodded. "Then we're ready."

Torlan looked out across the plateau.

The light had shifted.

Not dramatically.

But enough.

The reflective panels caught it differently now.

Sharper.

More defined.

"Adjust two degrees," Torlan said.

Darren followed his gaze.

Then moved.

A slight shift.

The reflected light intensified.

"Better," Darren said.

"Yes."

Silas leaned back slightly. "I'm starting to think this whole communication thing might be important."

No one responded.

Alex turned back toward the injured.

"Status?" she asked.

Lena looked up. "Stable. But they're not improving."

"They won't," Alex said. "We just hold them."

That was the truth of it.

They had traded danger for time.

Nothing more.

Gideon moved toward the perimeter.

"Keep rotation tight," he said. "No one drifts too far."

Tarin stood on the outer edge, scanning.

"There," he said quietly.

Heads turned.

At first—

Nothing.

Just sky.

Clear.

Wide.

Then—

A flicker.

Movement.

Far.

High.

Silas narrowed his eyes. "That it?"

"Yes," Tarin said.

The craft passed across the sky.

Fast.

Not descending.

Not searching randomly.

Following a pattern.

"They won't see us on the first pass," Darren said.

"No," Torlan replied.

The craft moved beyond them.

Disappeared behind a distant rise.

"Now?" Silas asked.

Torlan looked at the sky.

Measured the angle.

The light.

The timing.

"Prepare fire," he said.

Silas moved immediately.

Gathered the material.

Positioned it.

"Not yet," Torlan said.

Silas paused.

Then nodded.

Minutes passed.

The sky remained empty.

Then—

The craft returned.

Lower.

Slower.

"Now," Torlan said.

The fire lit quickly.

Dry material catching fast.

Smoke rising.

Not thick.

But visible.

Darren adjusted the reflective panels.

The light flashed.

Bright.

Directed.

The craft shifted.

Slightly.

"They see it," Tarin said.

The craft angled.

Not toward them.

Not directly.

But enough.

Alex lifted the receiver.

"Meridian, this is Hale. Visual contact with aircraft. Confirm."

The response came back.

Clear.

Immediate.

"…confirmed…visual acquired…marking position…ground team adjusting route…"

Gideon exhaled.

Slow.

Controlled.

Silas smiled faintly. "That's a good sign."

"Yes," Torlan said.

The craft passed overhead once more.

Closer now.

Lower.

Then—

Gone.

"They know where we are," Alex said.

Torlan nodded.

"Yes."

Darren powered down the signal slightly.

"Conserve energy," he said.

The fire burned lower.

Controlled.

The plateau settled again.

But something had changed.

Not the terrain.

Not the conditions.

The distance between them and rescue—

Had closed.

And now—

It was only a matter of time.

## Chapter 27 - Plateau Pressure

The plateau gave them space.

It did not give them comfort.

By mid-day, the heat had settled in.

Not extreme.

But constant.

The kind that pulled moisture slowly, steadily, without urgency—and without mercy.

Alex felt it first in the injured.

"Lena," she said quietly, "we increase rotation."

Lena looked up. "For shade?"

"Yes."

The sun had shifted higher.

What little natural cover the rock formations provided had begun to move with it, leaving sections of the camp exposed for longer than before.

They adjusted.

Again.

"Rotate every twenty minutes," Alex said. "No one stays in direct sun longer than that."

Lena nodded. "Water?"

"Still controlled," Alex replied. "But we adjust frequency. Smaller amounts. More often."

The tradeoff was immediate.

More hydration.

Faster depletion.

Gideon stepped in. "How long does that buy us?"

Alex didn't hesitate.

"Less than before."

Silas let out a quiet breath. "That's encouraging."

"No," Darren said. "That's reality."

Torlan stood near the edge of the rise, watching the terrain beyond their immediate camp.

Not idle.

Never idle.

The plateau stretched farther than it had appeared from below.

Shallow ridges.

Broken stone.

Low growth.

Nothing that offered easy travel.

Nothing that offered easy resources.

Tarin joined him.

"Not much out there," he said.

"No."

"Could be water somewhere."

"Yes."

"Too far to risk."

"Yes."

That settled it.

Darren approached from the signal unit.

"Power holding," he said. "But not indefinitely."

Torlan looked at him.

"How long?"

Darren considered.

"Two days with conservation," he said. "Three if we reduce transmissions."

Torlan nodded once.

"We reduce."

The decision moved quickly.

Shorter transmissions.

Fewer checks.

No unnecessary signal use.

Silas looked at the unit. "Feels strange to not use the one thing that's actually working."

"It's working because we're not overusing it," Darren said.

Silas nodded slowly. "Fair."

A sound broke across the plateau.

Not sharp.

Not immediate.

Carried by distance.

Everyone turned.

It came again.

Low.

Familiar.

"Those things again," Silas said quietly.

Tarin listened.

Head slightly tilted.

"They're below," he said.

"Yes," Torlan replied.

The sound moved.

Not circling.

Not probing.

Traveling.

"They're not coming up," Gideon said.

"No," Torlan said.

Silas exhaled. "Good."

But the sound remained.

Faint.

Persistent.

A reminder.

Alex moved back toward the injured.

One of them had shifted.

Breathing uneven.

She knelt.

Checked pulse.

Then looked up.

"He's slipping," she said.

The words landed.

Quietly.

Heavily.

Lena moved immediately. "What do you need?"

"Position change," Alex said. "Slight elevation. Keep him conscious."

Torlan stepped closer.

"How long?"

Alex didn't answer right away.

Then—

"He needs help we don't have."

Gideon's jaw tightened slightly.

"How long?"

Alex met his gaze.

"Not long enough to wait comfortably," she said.

That changed the timeline.

Torlan looked toward the horizon.

Then back at the signal.

Then at the group.

"We hold," he said.

Not because it was easy.

Because it was necessary.

The group adjusted again.

Not dramatically.

But inward.

Closer.

More focused.

Silas sat beside one of the injured, not speaking.

Just present.

Darren remained near the signal, checking, recalibrating, conserving.

Tarin moved along the outer edge, still scanning.

Still watching.

Gideon stood at the center.

Not directing.

Holding.

Alex worked.

Quiet.

Precise.

Torlan remained at the edge.

Looking out.

The plateau stretched ahead.

Unchanged.

Unforgiving.

The canyon below—

Hidden.

But still there.

The sky above—

Clear.

For now.

The sounds from below faded slowly.

Not gone.

Just distant.

And as the day moved forward—

A different kind of pressure settled in.

Not from the environment.

Not from the terrain.

From time.

They had escaped the canyon.

Now—

They had to outlast it.

## Chapter 28 - The Search Tightens

The second pass came sooner.

Not by much.

But enough.

Tarin saw it first.

"Movement," he said quietly.

Heads turned.

The sky was clearer now.

The light sharper.

The reflective panels caught it cleanly.

Then—

The craft.

Lower this time.

Slower.

Silas stood. "That's closer."

"Yes," Torlan said.

The craft adjusted its path.

Not sweeping wide now.

Focused.

"They're narrowing," Darren said.

Torlan watched the angle.

The speed.

The pattern.

"They have our coordinates," he said.

"Yes," Gideon replied.

"Prepare signal," Torlan said.

Silas was already moving.

The fire was ready.

Set.

Controlled.

"Wait," Torlan said.

Silas paused.

The craft shifted.

Slightly.

Then again.

"Now," Torlan said.

The fire ignited.

Quick.

Clean.

Smoke rose.

Thinner than before.

But visible.

Darren adjusted the panels.

Light flashed.

Sharp.

Deliberate.

The craft angled.

This time—

Directly.

"They see us," Tarin said.

The sound reached them seconds later.

Low.

Distant.

But real.

Silas smiled. "That's the best sound I've heard all week."

The craft passed over them.

Close enough now to feel.

Then—

It circled.

Not wide.

Tight.

Controlled.

Alex lifted the receiver.

"Meridian, this is Hale. Aircraft overhead. Confirm."

The response came instantly.

"…confirmed…visual lock established…ground team within range…adjusting approach…"

Gideon stepped forward. "How close?"

Alex listened.

Then—

"Hours," she said.

That changed everything.

Not relief.

Not yet.

Focus.

Torlan turned toward the group.

"We prepare for arrival," he said.

Gideon nodded. "Landing zone?"

Tarin stepped forward. "There," he said, pointing to a flatter section of plateau several meters out.

"Clear enough," he added. "But not perfect."

"Nothing here is," Silas said.

Torlan moved toward the area.

Others followed.

"Clear it," Gideon said. "Loose stone. Anything that can shift."

They worked.

Quickly.

Rocks moved.

Debris shifted.

Space opened.

Not large.

But enough.

Darren stepped beside Torlan.

"Aircraft won't land here," he said.

"No."

"Ground team will."

"Yes."

Silas looked toward the horizon. "Then we make it easy for them."

The space took shape.

Alex returned to the injured.

"They go first," she said.

Lena nodded. "All of them?"

"All we can move safely," Alex replied.

The reality of that settled in.

Torlan stepped back.

Looked across the plateau.

The canyon below remained hidden.

The plateau—

Now active.

The craft passed overhead again.

Lower.

Slower.

"They're guiding them in," Darren said.

"Yes," Torlan replied.

The sound faded.

Then returned.

From farther out.

Different.

Not air.

Ground.

Tarin turned.

Listening.

"You hear that?" he said.

Silas tilted his head.

Then nodded.

"Engines," he said.

Low.

Distant.

But growing.

Gideon exhaled.

Slow.

"They're coming," he said.

Torlan nodded once.

"Yes."

The group held position.

Not scattered.

Not uncertain.

Ready.

The plateau stretched ahead.

No longer empty.

And for the first time—

Rescue was not a promise.

It was approaching.

## Chapter 29 - The Waiting Line

The sound did not arrive all at once.

It built.

Slowly.

At first, it was only a low vibration beneath the wind—easy to miss if you weren't listening for it.

But they were.

All of them.

Tarin stood at the edge of the cleared landing area, head slightly turned, tracking the direction.

"Two vehicles," he said. "Maybe three."

Silas shaded his eyes, though there was nothing yet to see. "I'll take two if they get here faster."

Gideon didn't respond.

He was already moving through the group.

"Final check," he said. "Everything ready. No delays when they arrive."

The camp tightened.

Not from fear.

From focus.

Alex moved between the injured.

"Stay with me," she said quietly to one of them. "We're close now."

The man's eyes opened slightly.

Not fully.

But enough.

Lena adjusted the support under his shoulders.
"He's holding," she said.
"For now," Alex replied.

Torlan stood near the edge of the plateau, looking out toward the direction of the sound.
Still nothing visible.
But the pattern had changed.
The vibration was steadier now.
Closer.

"They're navigating the ridges," Darren said, stepping up beside him.
"Yes."
"Slower than I expected."
Torlan nodded.
"The terrain decides speed."

Silas glanced back toward the canyon.
The fog had thinned slightly along the upper edges, but the depth remained hidden.
"Good thing they're not coming from that direction," he muttered.

Tarin didn't look away from the horizon. "They wouldn't," he said.
"No?" Silas asked.
"No," Tarin replied. "Not if they know what they're doing."

Gideon returned to the center.
"All right," he said. "Positions."

The group shifted.
Not dramatically.
But into readiness.

Carriers moved into place beside the injured.
Darren checked the signal one last time.

Stable.

Holding.

Alex stood at the front of the medical group.

Watching.

Waiting.

The sound grew louder.

Then—

Movement.

A shape appeared along the far edge of the plateau.

Low.

Angular.

Dust trailing behind it.

"There," Tarin said.

The first vehicle crested a shallow rise.

Not fast.

Not aggressive.

Controlled.

Silas let out a breath. "That's real."

A second vehicle followed.

Then a third.

"They brought more than we expected," Gideon said.

Torlan watched the approach.

Measured.

"Prepared," he said.

The vehicles moved carefully across the uneven ground, adjusting for slope and surface, never pushing speed beyond control.

As they drew closer, details became clear.

Reinforced frames.

Wide tires.

Stabilized suspension.

Built for this terrain.

"Good machines," Darren said.

"Better operators," Tarin added.

The lead vehicle slowed.

Then stopped at a distance.

A moment passed.

Then the side hatch opened.

A figure stepped out.

Helmeted.

Controlled.

He raised one hand.

Not a wave.

A signal.

Torlan stepped forward.

Returned it.

The distance closed.

The rescue team moved with purpose.

Not rushed.

Not hesitant.

As they approached, the leader removed his helmet.

Older.

Weathered.

Eyes that had seen terrain like this before.

He looked at Torlan.

Measured him.

Then nodded once.

"You held position," he said.

"Yes," Torlan replied.

The man glanced at the group.

The injured.

The setup.

The signal markers.

"Well done," he said.

Gideon stepped forward. "We've got critical cases," he said.

The rescuer nodded. "We move them first."

No wasted words.

No unnecessary questions.

The team spread out immediately.

Two moved to the stretchers.

Another began assessing the ground for loading stability.

One remained near the vehicles.

Watching.

Alex stepped in beside them.

"Careful with this one," she said. "He's borderline."

The rescuer nodded. "We'll stabilize en route."

Lena stepped back.

Just enough.

Silas watched the movement.

Then shook his head slightly.

"They make it look easy."

Darren replied quietly. "It's not."

The first stretcher lifted.

Not improvised now.

Supported.

Secured.

The group watched.

Not speaking.

The distance between survival—

And rescue—

Closed with every step.

Torlan remained still.

Watching.

The canyon behind them.

The plateau ahead.

The team moving between.

For the first time—

They were no longer alone.

They were being brought back.

## Chapter 30 - The Extraction Begins

They did not rush the loading.

That was the difference.

The rescue team moved with speed—

But not urgency.

Every action deliberate.

Every motion controlled.

"Stabilize here," the lead rescuer said, indicating a slightly lower section of ground beside the first vehicle.

Two of his team adjusted immediately.

They set a support frame.

Locked it.

Checked it.

"Bring him in," he said.

The stretcher moved.

Not improvised now.

Guided.

Alex walked beside it.

Watching every movement.

"Easy," she said. "Keep him level."

The rescuer glanced at her. "We've got him."

She didn't step away.

Not yet.

They secured the stretcher into the vehicle.

Locked.

Checked.

Then checked again.

"Next," the rescuer said.

The second injured came forward.

Behind them, the group remained still.

Not waiting idly.

Observing.

Gideon stood at the center.

Watching the sequence.

Learning the pattern.

"They've done this before," Silas said quietly.

"Yes," Darren replied.

Torlan remained near the edge of the landing area.

Watching everything.

Not intervening.

Not directing.

The system had changed.

And he let it.

The third stretcher lifted.

This one more stable.

Less critical.

Still handled with care.

Lena stepped forward briefly. "Watch his shoulder," she said.

The rescuer nodded. "Noted."

The stretcher secured.

The vehicles adjusted slightly.

Not repositioning fully.

Just enough.

"Two more in this unit," one of the team called.

The lead rescuer nodded. "We cycle."

Gideon stepped forward. "How many runs?"

"Two," the rescuer replied.

"Maybe three if we take equipment."

Gideon considered that.

Then nodded.

"People first," he said.

"Always," the rescuer replied.

Silas glanced at Darren. "I like these guys."

Darren didn't answer.

He was watching the vehicle systems.

Tracking.

Learning.

The first vehicle powered up.

Low.

Controlled.

"Clear path," the driver called.

The team stepped back.

The vehicle moved.

Not fast.

Not slow.

Deliberate.

It turned.

Aligned with the terrain.

Then began its descent along a route that had not been visible from above.

Silas watched it go. "They found a path we didn't."

"Yes," Tarin said.

"They had time."

The second vehicle moved forward.

"Next group," the rescuer called.

This time—

Not stretchers.

"Walking wounded first," Gideon said.

Alex nodded. "Those who can move safely."

They formed.

Carefully.

Supported.

Torlan stepped forward.

A man near the rear of the group hesitated.

Unsteady.

Torlan reached him.

Without comment.

Lifted.

Not a full carry.

Not a strain.

Just—

Support.

Complete.

The man steadied immediately.

Silas saw it.

So did Darren.

So did Gideon.

None of them spoke.

The second group moved.

Loaded.

Secured.

The vehicle adjusted.

Prepared.

"Final check," the rescuer said.

Alex stepped forward.

Looked at each one.

Then nodded.

"Go."

The second vehicle moved.

Now only one remained.

The plateau felt larger again.

Quieter.

Gideon looked around.

Counting.

"We're almost there," he said.

Lena exhaled slowly.

"Almost."

The final group gathered.

Darren secured the signal unit.

Powered it down.

Carefully.

Silas picked up what remained of their supplies.

Less than before.

More than they had expected.

Tarin scanned the horizon one last time.

Torlan turned.

Looked back.

The canyon remained hidden beneath the fog.

Unchanged.

But no longer part of their path.

The final vehicle powered up.

"Load," the rescuer said.

They moved.

One by one.

Torlan stepped in last.

The door closed.

The engine rose.

The plateau shifted beneath them as the vehicle began to move.

Not away.

Forward.

Toward home.

# Chapter 31 - The Ride Back

Chapter 31 - The Ride Back

The vehicle did not move quickly.

That was the first thing they noticed.

Not because it lacked power.

Because speed did not belong here.

The ground shifted constantly beneath them.

Rock gave way to loose gravel.

Gravel to hard-packed ridges.

Ridges to shallow drops that required careful descent before climbing again.

The driver didn't rush any of it.

Hands steady.

Eyes forward.

Adjusting.

Always adjusting.

Inside, the motion translated differently.

Not violent.

But persistent.

A constant reminder that the terrain still mattered.

"Suspension's doing most of the work," Darren said quietly, watching the system readouts.

The rescuer across from him glanced up. "It has to," he said. "Or we don't make it."

Silas leaned back slightly, then thought better of it and braced instead. "I'm starting to appreciate why you didn't come down faster," he said.

"We came as fast as the ground allowed," the rescuer replied.

Alex remained near the injured.

Her attention hadn't shifted since they were loaded.

"Stay with me," she said again, checking pulse, breathing, response.

One of the men stirred slightly.

A good sign.

Lena mirrored her movements.

Less uncertain now.

More confident.

Gideon sat across from them.

Watching.

Not intervening.

Trusting.

Torlan sat near the rear of the vehicle.

Not resting.

Observing.

The plateau passed around them in uneven patterns.

The same terrain they had stood on—

Now seen in motion.

Tarin leaned slightly toward one of the side panels, watching the route unfold.

"You're taking a different line than I expected," he said.

The driver nodded. "Less direct," he said. "More stable."

"That makes sense," Tarin replied.

Silas glanced between them. "Everything makes sense when you've already done it once."

Darren looked at the route ahead.
Then back at the plateau behind them.
"We would've found something," he said.

"Yes," Torlan said.

Silas smirked faintly. "Probably not this."

No one argued.

The vehicle crested a low ridge.
Then angled downward.
Carefully.

The injured shifted slightly.
Alex steadied them immediately.
"Slow that descent," she said.

The driver adjusted.
Without question.

"Better?" he asked.

"Yes."

The vehicle leveled.
Then continued.

Time passed.
Not measured.
Felt.

The plateau gave way slowly.
Not to easier ground.
To known ground.

The terrain began to change.
Subtle at first.
Then clear.

More defined paths.
Less fractured rock.
Wider spaces between obstacles.

Silas noticed first.

"This looks… better," he said.

"Yes," the rescuer replied.

Gideon leaned forward slightly.

"How far?" he asked.

"Another hour," the rescuer said.

Silas exhaled. "That's the best thing I've heard today."

Darren didn't respond.

He was watching the systems.

Still learning.

Still processing.

Torlan remained still.

Not withdrawn.

Present.

The motion of the vehicle did not distract him.

The change in terrain did not relax him.

Not yet.

Alex checked the injured again.

"He's holding," she said quietly.

Lena nodded.

"Barely," she added.

That was enough.

The vehicle continued.

The sky shifted above them.

Not dramatically.

But enough to mark time.

The plateau behind them faded.

The canyon—

Gone entirely now.

Ahead—

Something new.

The outline of structures.

Far.

But visible.

Silas leaned forward.

"That's it, isn't it?"

"Yes," the rescuer said.

Gideon looked at Torlan.

Then back at the horizon.

"Outpost Meridian," he said.

Torlan nodded once.

"Yes."

The vehicle didn't speed up.

Didn't rush the final stretch.

It didn't need to.

They were already there.

They just had to arrive.

## Chapter 32 - Arrival

The outpost did not rise suddenly into view.

It appeared gradually, as if the land itself had decided to give it back to them piece by piece.

At first, it was only shape.

Lines against the horizon that did not belong to rock or ridge. Straight edges. Angles that held their form no matter how the terrain shifted.

Then color.

Muted metal. Structured surfaces. Something built with intention.

Silas leaned forward slightly, bracing himself as the vehicle moved over another uneven stretch. "I'll admit," he said, "that's a good sight."

No one disagreed.

Gideon's eyes stayed fixed on the structures as they grew larger. "Perimeter looks intact," he said quietly.

Tarin nodded. "No damage. No emergency activity."

"That's good," Alex said, though her attention never fully left the injured.

Torlan watched in silence.

Not because there was nothing to say.

Because this moment did not require it.

The vehicle continued its steady approach, adjusting for terrain, never rushing the final distance.

As they drew closer, more detail emerged.

Outer barriers.

Landing platforms.

Communication towers rising above the main structures.

Movement.

People.

Waiting.

They had been seen.

The vehicle slowed further.

Not because of difficulty.

Because they were entering controlled space.

A signal passed between the vehicle and the outpost—unseen, but understood. The gates ahead began to open.

Silas let out a breath. "That's the best sound I've heard yet."

Darren watched the sequence carefully. "Automated response," he said. "But coordinated."

"Yes," Torlan replied.

The vehicle passed through the outer gate.

Inside, the ground changed immediately.

Stabilized.

Level.

Constructed.

After everything they had crossed, the difference was almost jarring.

The motion of the vehicle smoothed.

Not completely.

But enough.

Alex adjusted her position beside the injured as the change in movement shifted their weight slightly. "Easy," she said. "We're almost there."

The man closest to her opened his eyes briefly.

This time, there was recognition.

Lena saw it too and gave a small nod. "He knows," she said quietly.

"Yes," Alex replied.

The vehicle came to a controlled stop.

The door opened.

Light shifted.

Voices.

Not urgent.

Prepared.

A medical team was already in place.

They moved forward immediately, not asking questions they already had answers to.

"Transfer on three," one of them said.

They lifted the first stretcher.

Smooth.

Practiced.

Gone within seconds toward the medical bay.

Alex stepped out with them, walking alongside, continuing her assessment even as the outpost team took over.

"Internal trauma," she said. "Watch pressure."

"We've got it," the medic replied.

Lena followed.

Not as an assistant now.

As part of the process.

Inside the vehicle, the remaining group began to move.

Gideon stepped down first, then turned to help the next person out without thinking about it.

Silas followed, pausing once his feet hit stable ground. He looked down at it, then gave a small shake of his head. "I'm not taking this for granted again," he said.

Darren stepped out next, his attention already shifting to the surrounding systems. He took in the structure, the layout, the flow of people.

Learning.

Always learning.

Tarin followed, scanning the perimeter instinctively before allowing himself to fully step away from the vehicle.

Torlan stepped down last.

He paused for a moment, not from hesitation, but from awareness.

The movement.

The order.

The structure.

All of it functioning.

He stepped forward.

Gideon looked at him. "We made it," he said.

Torlan nodded once. "Yes."

There was no need to say more.

Around them, the outpost moved efficiently.

No panic.

No confusion.

Only response.

The remaining injured were carried in.

The last of the equipment removed.

The vehicle cleared.

Silas watched it go. "Feels strange not needing that anymore."

"You needed it," Darren said. "You just don't need it now."

Silas nodded slowly. “I can live with that.”

Across the open area, Alex turned briefly, looking back toward the group.

Not checking.

Confirming.

Torlan met her gaze.

A slight nod passed between them.

Understood.

They had crossed the canyon.

Climbed the wall.

Held the plateau.

Now—

They had returned.

And for the first time since the crash, the next step was no longer survival.

It was recovery.

## Chapter 33 – Recovery

The outpost moved on without them.

That was the first thing they noticed.

Not because they were unimportant.

Because the system worked.

Medical teams moved quickly through the injured.

Doors opened and closed with purpose.

Voices carried—not urgent, not strained—just clear.

Each person taken where they needed to go.

No delay.

No confusion.

Alex remained inside.

That was expected.

She did not step away from the injured when others took over.

She transitioned with them.

Adjusted.

Stayed involved.

Lena stayed with her.

Not because she had to.

Because she belonged there now.

Outside, the group gathered near the edge of the intake area.

Not directed.

Not dismissed.

Just… waiting.

Silas shifted his weight slightly, then stopped and looked down again.

Still steady ground.

Still real.

"I keep expecting this to move," he said.

"It won't," Darren replied.

Silas gave a small nod. "Good."

Gideon stood a short distance away, watching the flow of personnel.

He wasn't analyzing it.

Not fully.

He was measuring something else.

Consistency.

Reliability.

The absence of chaos.

"They've done this before," he said quietly.

Tarin followed his gaze. "Many times," he replied.

Darren glanced at the systems along the outer wall.

Communication relays.

Power lines.

Structured, integrated.

"This place holds," he said.

"Yes," Gideon replied.

Torlan stood slightly apart.

Not isolated.

Positioned.

He watched the movement.

The coordination.

The way each part connected to the next without hesitation.

A man approached.

Not rushed.

Not hesitant.

He stopped a few steps away.

"Torlan Tarsen," he said.

Not a question.

Torlan turned.

"Yes."

The man nodded once.

"Command has been informed," he said. "They'd like a report when you're ready."

Torlan held his gaze for a moment.

Then nodded.

"Yes."

The man looked past him briefly—at the group.

"They did well," he said.

"Yes," Torlan replied.

The man inclined his head slightly.

Then stepped away.

Silas looked over. "That sounded official."

"It was," Darren said.

Gideon turned slightly. "You're not surprised," he said to Torlan.

"No."

Gideon studied him for a moment.

Then nodded once.

"That makes sense."

The doors to the medical wing opened again.

Alex stepped out.

Her pace had changed.

Not slower.

Less urgent.

Lena followed.

Silas straightened. "How are they?"

Alex exhaled once.

"Stabilized," she said.

Relief moved through the group.

Not loudly.

But clearly.

Gideon nodded. "All of them?"

"Yes," Alex replied.

"Some closer than others."

That was enough truth.

Lena looked at them.

"They're asking about you," she said.

Silas blinked. "Already?"

"They're awake," Lena said.

Darren gave a small nod.

"That's good."

Tarin looked toward the medical wing.

"Means they made it through the worst of it," he said.

"Yes," Alex replied.

Torlan stepped forward slightly.

"Good," he said.

Alex met his gaze.

A moment passed.

Not words.

Recognition.

They had both carried the same weight.

In different ways.

Gideon stepped in.

"What's next?" he asked.

Alex looked toward the main structure.

"Rest," she said.

"Then report."

Silas let out a breath. "I like the sound of the first part."

Darren glanced at him. "You'll like the second part less."

Silas gave a faint smile. "I figured."

The group began to shift.

Not moving away.

Not dispersing.

Just… loosening.

The tension that had held them together for days did not vanish.

It eased.

Torlan turned slightly toward the central structure.

Gideon watched him.

"You'll go," he said.

"Yes."

Gideon nodded.

Silas looked between them. "Try not to get assigned anything else while we're here," he said.

Torlan did not respond.

But there was the faintest trace of something—

Almost a smile.

Across the outpost, the systems continued.

Unchanged.

Uninterrupted.

The canyon was behind them.

The plateau was behind them.

What remained—

Was what came next.

And for the first time—

They had the space to face it.

## Chapter 34 - The Report

The outpost was quieter away from the intake area.

Not silent.

But controlled.

Measured.

The movement of personnel continued, but without urgency. Systems functioned. Doors opened and closed. Information moved where it needed to go.

Everything had its place.

That was the difference.

Torlan walked beside Gideon through one of the main corridors, the sound of their steps steady against the reinforced floor.

"You've been here before," Gideon said.

"Yes."

Gideon glanced at him. "Recently?"

"No."

That was enough.

They continued.

The corridor opened into a larger room—functional, not decorative. A central table. Display surfaces along the far wall. Data already present, already waiting.

They were expected.

A small group stood near the table.

Not many.

That mattered.

This wasn't a formal inquiry.

It was something more direct.

The man who stepped forward was older, composed, carrying the kind of authority that didn't need to announce itself.

"Torlan Tarsen," he said.

Torlan inclined his head slightly. "Yes."

The man nodded. "I'm Commander Halev."

He glanced briefly at Gideon. "You're Trask."

"Yes."

"Good," Halev said. "We'll keep this simple."

That, too, mattered.

No ceremony.

No delay.

"Walk me through it," Halev said.

Torlan did not sit.

He stood at the table, looking down at the display as it shifted to show terrain mapping of the canyon region.

"The vessel went down here," he said, indicating the crash site. "Descent was controlled, but compromised by environmental interference."

Halev nodded once. "We've reviewed partial telemetry. Continue."

"The canyon restricted signal," Torlan said. "Distortion increased with depth. Communication failed repeatedly."

Gideon stepped in. "Initial priority was survival and stabilization," he said. "We secured the area, treated injuries, attempted signal repair."

Halev's attention shifted between them.

"Casualties?"

"Five," Gideon said.

Halev acknowledged it with a slight nod.

"Continue."

Torlan indicated the lower region of the canyon. "Environmental factors compounded risk. Visibility loss. Signal degradation. Predator presence."

Halev's expression didn't change. "Confirmed," he said. "We've logged similar activity in that region."

Gideon glanced at him. "Would have been useful information."

"It was restricted," Halev replied calmly.

That was not an apology.

It didn't need to be.

Torlan continued. "Decision was made to relocate."

Halev looked at him more directly. "Your decision."

"Yes."

"Based on?"

"Pattern observation," Torlan said. "Signal failure would not resolve at that depth. Rescue access limited. Risk increasing."

Halev held his gaze for a moment.

Then nodded.

"Continue."

Gideon spoke next. "We executed staged ascent. Established positions. Rotated carriers. Managed injuries during movement."

Halev glanced at the terrain model as it updated, highlighting the route.

"That path is not obvious," he said.

"No," Torlan replied.

Halev looked back at him.

"But it worked."

"Yes."

Halev nodded once.

Torlan continued. "Reached plateau. Signal restored to functional level. Visual markers deployed. Contact established."

Halev looked at the final position on the map.

Then at them.

"Rescue team reported your setup was… efficient," he said.

Gideon allowed the faintest shift in expression. "We adapted."

"Yes," Halev said.

He stepped back slightly from the table.

"That's clear."

The room settled.

Not silent.

Complete.

Halev looked between them once more.

"You held structure under pressure," he said. "That's what kept you alive."

Neither of them responded.

They didn't need to.

Halev inclined his head slightly. "You'll both file formal reports," he said. "But this—" he gestured lightly toward the display "—is sufficient."

Gideon nodded. "Understood."

Halev looked at Torlan.

"There are those who suggested bringing you in," he said. "It appears they were correct."

Torlan didn't answer immediately.

Then—

"Yes."

Halev watched him for a moment.

Then gave a small nod.

"Rest," he said. "You've earned it."

The meeting ended without ceremony.

No dismissal.

No formal close.

Just completion.

Torlan turned.

Gideon followed.

They stepped back into the corridor.

For a few moments, neither spoke.

Then—

"You knew it would come to that," Gideon said.

"Yes."

Gideon glanced at him. "The decision to move."

"Yes."

Gideon exhaled slowly.

"I didn't," he said.

Torlan didn't respond.

Gideon looked ahead as they walked.

"But I followed it," he added.

"Yes."

That was enough.

They reached the junction where the corridor split.

Medical one direction.

Living quarters the other.

Gideon paused.

"Get some rest," he said.

Torlan inclined his head once.

"You too."

Gideon turned and walked toward the quarters.

Torlan remained a moment longer.

Then turned toward medical.

Not because he was needed.

Because he was not finished.

The outpost moved around him.

Steady.

Reliable.

Structured.

And for the first time since the crash—

The decisions were no longer immediate.

But they still mattered.

## Epilogue - After the Climb

The outpost was quieter at night.

Not silent.

Never silent.

But the movement slowed, the voices softened, and the steady rhythm of systems settled into something that no longer demanded attention.

It simply continued.

William stood alone on the outer platform.

The air was cooler now.

The wind lighter.

The plateau stretched out before him, fading into shadow where the land dipped and rose beyond the reach of the outpost lights.

Farther still—

The canyon.

It was there.

He could see the shape of it now, even in the dark.

Not clearly.

But enough.

It no longer felt like something waiting.

It felt like something that had already happened.

Footsteps approached behind him.

He didn't turn.

"You always end up here," Alex said.

"Yes."

She stepped beside him, folding her arms lightly against the night air.

For a moment, she didn't speak.

She simply looked out across the same ground.

"It looks different at night," she said.

"Yes."

"Less… defined."

"Yes."

She nodded slightly.

"But it's still there."

"Yes."

That was enough.

They stood in silence.

Not empty.

Not searching.

Just—

Present.

After a moment, Alex spoke again.

"They're all going to recover," she said.

William nodded once.

"Yes."

"And the others?" she asked.

He knew what she meant.

"They will as well," he said.

She accepted that.

Not because it was certain.

Because it was the direction.

A faint movement of light passed across the distant terrain—one of the outpost patrol units moving along its route.

Steady.

Unhurried.

Reliable.

Alex let out a slow breath.

"We made it," she said.

William didn't answer immediately.

Then—

"Yes."

There was no need to say more than that.

After a moment, she turned slightly toward him.

"William," she said.

He looked at her.

"Yes."

She studied him for just a second.

Not questioning.

Recognizing.

"You didn't change," she said.

A pause.

Then—

"I did," he replied.

She considered that.

Then smiled.

"Maybe," she said.

They stood there a little longer.

The wind moving gently across the platform.

The outpost steady behind them.

The land open before them.

At last, Alex stepped back.

"Get some rest," she said.

"Yes."

She turned and walked toward the interior.

Not hurried.

Not reluctant.

William remained where he was.

He looked out across the plateau one more time.

Then toward the canyon.

Then beyond it.

What had happened there would remain.

Not as something unfinished.

Not as something unresolved.

As something learned.

He turned.

The platform lights guided the way back inside.

Behind him, the night held steady.

And for the first time since the crash—

There was nothing pressing forward.

Nothing demanding an answer.

Only what had been done.

And what would come—

In its time.

## Author's Note

Stories like this often begin with a simple idea—
a journey into the unknown.

But along the way, they become something more.

*The Canyon Ascent* is not just about a difficult path through a harsh and uncertain place. It is about the quiet decisions made when the way forward is unclear… when the ground is unstable… and when turning back would be easier.

Torlan and his team faced more than terrain. They faced the need to trust one another, to act with care rather than haste, and to keep moving forward even when progress felt slow.

Those moments, I believe, are familiar to all of us.

Not every challenge announces itself.
Not every answer comes quickly.
And sometimes the most important step is simply the next one.

If this story has reminded you of the value of patience, of steady leadership, or of standing together when things are uncertain—then it has done what I hoped it would do.

Thank you for taking this journey.

There is more ahead.

—Russell McFall

## A Torlan Tarsen Adventure

The Torlan Tarsen series follows a seasoned leader and those who journey alongside him as they face the challenges of unfamiliar worlds, difficult terrain, and the unknown forces that shape them.

Each story is grounded in exploration, problem-solving, and the quiet strength required to move forward when certainty is out of reach.

These are not tales of reckless action, but of careful decisions—of people who choose patience over panic, precision over impulse, and teamwork over isolation.

In every mission, the environment is more than a backdrop.
It is a test.

And in every test, what matters most is not just survival—
but how the journey is faced.

# Appendix — Canyon Incident Summary

**Classification:** Internal Mission Record
**Mission Segment:** Canyon Descent and Extraction
**Status:** Completed

---

### 1. Operational Overview

Following the uncontrolled descent of the transport vessel, personnel were forced to evacuate into an uncharted canyon environment.
Initial conditions included limited visibility, unstable terrain, and no confirmed extraction route.
All movement beyond the crash site required on-site assessment and decision-making without external guidance.
Primary objective shifted from transit to survival and controlled ascent.

---

### 2. Environmental Conditions

The canyon presented a series of compounding hazards:

- Dense fog layers reducing long-range visibility
- Sheer rock walls limiting directional movement
- Unstable ground sections with shifting surfaces
- Narrow passages restricting group movement

Light conditions varied significantly throughout the canyon, creating intermittent zones of clarity and obstruction.
No established pathways or natural exit routes were identified at initial survey.

---

### 3. Structural and Terrain Observations

The canyon walls displayed significant vertical variation, with limited natural formations suitable for ascent.

Key observations included:

- Intermittent ledges providing temporary positioning points
- Irregular rock formations allowing controlled upward movement
- Sections of compressed debris that appeared stable but required testing

Progress required continuous evaluation of surface integrity and route viability.

---

**4. Decision Path and Movement Strategy**

Movement through the canyon was conducted using a controlled, step-based approach:

- Advance only after confirming stability of each position
- Maintain visual and physical awareness between individuals
- Avoid rapid progression in favor of sustained, reliable movement

Multiple potential routes were evaluated and dismissed due to risk factors.

Final ascent path was selected based on cumulative assessment rather than initial visibility.

---

**5. Personnel Coordination**

Successful navigation of the canyon required consistent communication and trust between individuals.

Key coordination factors:

- Shared observation and real-time input
- Immediate response to environmental changes
- Willingness to pause, reassess, and adjust direction

No independent movement was executed outside of group awareness.

---

**6. Outcome**

All personnel successfully exited the canyon environment.

No additional loss of life occurred following initial descent.

Primary objective—safe extraction—was achieved through:

- Measured decision-making
- Controlled movement
- Sustained group coordination

---

**7. Final Assessment**

The canyon environment presented no single solution or direct route to safety.

Successful ascent was achieved through:

- Incremental progress
- Careful evaluation of each step
- Collective discipline under uncertain conditions

---

**8. Closing Observation**

Not all paths are visible at the beginning.

In this instance, progress was not defined by speed, but by steadiness.

Each step, once confirmed, made the next possible.

## About the Author

Russell McFall writes thoughtful, clean science fiction focused on teamwork, perseverance, and steady leadership. His stories grew from years of telling adventures to his children and continue to reflect a deep belief in character, purpose, and doing what is right—especially when the path is uncertain.

## Also by Russell McFall

*Ordained Path Books*

Clean Science Fiction and Inspirational Writing for Thoughtful Readers

---

### A Torlan Tarsen Adventure

- *Character-driven science fiction of leadership, problem-solving, and quiet strength*
- **Torlan Tarsen — Raised Among Giants**
- **Torlan Tarsen — The Havenfall Accord**
- **Torlan Tarsen — The Lost Expedition — Asterra-9**
- **Torlan Tarsen — The Canyon Ascent**

---

### Contemporary Fiction and Short Stories

Stories of Community, Memory, and Hope

- **Squirrel Creek Estates — Where the Porch Lights Stay On**
- **The World That Chose**

---

### The Space Cadet Richard Series

*Where the Legacy Began*

- **The Final Countdown**
- **The Dunes of Dinkytown**
- **The Mastermind's Maze**

---

### The Space Cadet Legacy Series

*Over 30+ novels of courage, friendship, and discovery — including*

- **The First Gate**

- **Welcome Back, Player**
- **Flibber's Journey Home**
- **Stronger Together**
- **Phasegate Rising**
- **The Makers' Handshake**
- **Optimized**

*(New missions continuing.)*

---

**Literary Humor and Reflections**

**Serious Nonsense — Sanity Sold Separately**

---

**Devotional and Reflection Books**

- **Remembering God's Help — Stone by Stone**
- **Attributes of God**
- **This Is My Story, This Is My Song**
- **Lives of Faith**
- **Foundations of Faith**

---

Russell McFall writes clean fiction and thoughtful reflections designed to uplift the heart, sharpen the mind, and remind every reader that light still wins.

www.ingramcontent.com/pod-product-compliance
Lightning Source LLC
LaVergne TN
LVHW010646110826
845149LV00014B/2966
* 9 7 8 1 9 7 2 7 2 4 1 0 1 *